ALWAYS AND FOREVER

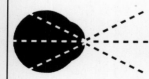

This Large Print Book carries the
Seal of Approval of N.A.V.H.

BAYOU DREAMS

ALWAYS AND FOREVER

FARRAH ROCHON

THORNDIKE PRESS
A part of Gale, Cengage Learning

GALE
CENGAGE Learning®

Farmington Hills, Mich • San Francisco • New York • Waterville, Maine
Meriden, Conn • Mason, Ohio • Chicago

GALE
CENGAGE Learning

Copyright © 2013 by Farrah Roybiskie.
Bayou Dreams Series.
Thorndike Press, a part of Gale, Cengage Learning.

Thorndike Press® Large Print African-American.
The text of this Large Print edition is unabridged.
Other aspects of the book may vary from the original edition.
Set in 16 pt. Plantin.

LIBRARY OF CONGRESS CATALOGING-IN-PUBLICATION DATA

Rochon, Farrah.
  Always and forever / by Farrah Rochon. — Large Print edition.
    pages cm. — (Bayou Dreams series) (Thorndike Press Large Print African-American)
    ISBN-13: 978-1-4104-6768-3 (hardcover)
    ISBN-10: 1-4104-6768-6 (hardcover)
    1. African Americans—Fiction. 2. Homecoming—Fiction. 3. Louisiana—Fiction. 4. Large type books. I. Title.
PS3618.O346A79 2014
813'.6—dc23   2013046805

Published in 2014 by arrangement with Harlequin Books S. A.

Printed in Mexico
1 2 3 4 5 6 7 18 17 16 15 14

For Jasmine Gabrielle Stewart, my favorite Disney cast member. I'm so proud of you.

Be strong and courageous . . . for the Lord your God is with you.

— *Deuteronomy* 31:6

Many thanks to my critique group member and dear friend Shauna Roberts. Your knowledge of historic properties saved me from many hours of tedious research.

And to Phyllis Bourne. Thanks for the encouraging daily text messages and endless supply of coffee. I owe you!

CHAPTER 1

The soulful strains of Irvin Mayfield's "7th Ward Blues" streaming from the iPod speakers were drowned out by the buzz saw as Jamal Johnson split a panel of Sheetrock lengthwise down the middle. He stacked the two pieces together and propped them against his truck's lowered tailgate, then placed another board on the saw table and repeated the process.

Jamal snatched the rag from his back pocket and mopped sweat from his brow. He'd lived in the small town of Gauthier, Louisiana, for over a year now, and he still wasn't used to this oppressive heat. Arizona saw its share of triple-digit highs, but the added humidity made the air here thick enough to choke on.

He hauled the drywall up the back porch steps of the 1870s Victorian he'd purchased a few months earlier, careful not to drag it. He gingerly navigated through the narrow

9

hallway and, when he reached the dining room, fitted the board against the exposed wall stud and positioned a nail. He slid the hammer from the holder on his tool belt, but it slipped from his fingers, crashing to the floor and tearing through the protective plastic sheeting.

"Dammit," Jamal bit out when he noticed the chip left in the hardwood flooring underneath. He tried to balance the drywall with one hand while stooping for the hammer, but his hand slipped and the Sheetrock fell forward. He hopped out of the way just before it could crash on top of him.

Jamal's head slumped in frustrated defeat as a puff of powdery dust floated up from where the drywall lay in a crumbly mess at his feet.

"Damn." He kneaded the bridge of his nose, praying the headache that had instantly sprouted behind his eyes would subside. But Jamal knew his troubles were far more complicated than the throbbing in his skull.

He was in over his head. *Way* over his head.

"Jamal?" called a voice from just beyond the doorway.

"Oh, great," Jamal muttered as his best friend's wife, Mya Dubois-Anderson, crossed the threshold. He forced a smile, hoping the strain of this latest debacle didn't show on his face.

"How's it . . ." Mya stopped short, eyeing the crumbled drywall. "Going?"

"It's going great," Jamal lied. "I was just about to get another piece of drywall. This one had a crack in it."

"Just one crack?" she asked, a skeptical brow arching in inquiry.

Jamal disregarded the mess on the floor with a nonchalant wave and motioned for Mya to follow him outside. He dusted off the porch step and aided her as she took a seat, taking care not to bump her very pregnant belly.

"So, how are things going with preparations for Christmas in Gauthier?" Jamal asked.

"It is going to be amazing," Mya said with the enthusiasm of a child who'd just won a shopping spree at a toy store. "That article in *Essence* magazine about the Louisiana African American Heritage Trail was the best publicity we could have ever asked for. The New City of Gauthier website is averaging five hundred hits a day. When do you think you'll have the website for Belle Maison up and running?"

The website? He was more concerned

with making sure the *house* would be up and running.

"The website should be done any day now," Jamal assured her, making a mental note to check with his web designer. "Although, not having a website hasn't stopped anyone from finding us. Belle Maison is already booked solid for the entire month-long celebration."

Mya visibly relaxed. "That is awesome news, Jamal. This bed-and-breakfast is vital to the civic association's long-term strategy for revitalizing the town." She winked at him. "Gauthier is lucky to have a world-class architect as a resident."

"World-class, huh? I don't know about that."

"Well, I do." She gave his forearm a gentle squeeze. "Seriously, Jamal. I cannot thank you enough. The one thing Gauthier is missing is lodging for visitors. Once this B&B opens, I just know the town is going to see a spike in tourists.

"I don't want to keep you away from work any longer," she said, rising from the porch step. "Now, you're sure Belle Maison will be ready by the start of the Christmas in Gauthier celebration, right?"

Jamal held his hand over his heart. "You have my word."

"That's good enough for me," Mya said, her smile bright and airy.

Jamal walked her to her car and waited until she'd backed out of the driveway before heading back to the disaster that awaited him in the dining room.

As he eyed the crumbled mess, Jamal grudgingly acknowledged that this stately home had gotten the better of him. His forte was designing homes; he wasn't used to the hammer-and-nails side of things. During the course of the past year, he'd definitely gained new respect for the laborers who'd worked for his family's company back in Arizona.

Unfortunately, he didn't have time to linger over this rebuild as he'd done with the house on Pecan Drive that he'd bought when he moved to Gauthier last year. If the slew of reservations wasn't enough to light a fire under his ass, the hope and excitement he'd just witnessed in Mya's eyes certainly was.

"You can't do this on your own." Jamal sighed.

He needed help. Pronto.

Jamal rubbed a distracted hand along the back of his neck, trying to ease the tension quickly building there. He knew whom he had to call, but God, he didn't want to call

13

her. Phylicia Phillips was the *last* person he wanted to bring in on this project. She was bossy and opinionated.

And she was so damn fine Jamal had counted at least four times that he'd nearly been caught staring at her ass when they had both stood as attendants two months ago at Corey and Mya's wedding.

He didn't know what had come over him, but after too many torturous hours of stealing glances at the way the satin bridesmaid gown had curved over her backside, his hand had taken on a mind of its own. He'd felt himself losing control, his palm inching forward to grab her behind. If the photographer hadn't called the wedding party for more pictures at the precise moment that his hand had nearly made contact, Jamal figured he'd still be sporting a black eye, courtesy of Phylicia's right hook.

If he closed his eyes, Jamal could recall every detail as she'd walked up the aisle of the church — from her hair, entwined with peach and white flowers, to the tips of her toes, peeking from underneath the gown's satiny hem. He'd been caught off guard, seeing her in a dress. Her usual attire was jeans and a T-shirt, often littered with wood shavings and other remnants from whatever project she was working on.

Phylicia Phillips was one of the most sought-after restoration specialists in this entire region. Earlier this year, he'd hired her to restore the banister in his house on Pecan Drive, and he still marveled at the job she'd done. She was the go-to woman when it came to finding old things and making them new, which was why he needed her for this job.

Jamal tipped his head back and expelled a strained sigh.

This would be so much easier if the woman didn't confuse the hell out of him!

He'd felt a spark from the first moment he met her, but she had never given him even an inkling that she felt the same way. Jamal thought everything had changed the night of Corey and Mya's wedding. After the reception, Phylicia had suggested they go out for coffee. They had gone to a 24/7 doughnut shop in neighboring Maplesville and spent hours talking about every topic under the sun.

Then nothing. Absolutely nothing.

When he'd called Phylicia the next day, she'd acted as if he were a stranger — one she didn't want to be bothered with. He would never understand women. And now he had to work with the most complicated one he'd ever met.

15

Could he survive working so closely with her?

"You don't have a choice," Jamal reminded himself. Even though he was updating the house with cutting-edge green technology, the 1870s Victorian had valuable woodwork that needed to be preserved. There was only one person who would give the amount of care and detail this project demanded.

Jamal dusted bits of drywall from his clothes as he headed for the black Ford F-150 he'd bought when he'd first moved to Gauthier — yet another stark change from his old life back in Phoenix. He'd driven a Lexus since he was a teenager. Every member of his family would probably fall away in a dead faint at the sight of him behind the wheel of a pickup truck.

Jamal popped open the glove compartment and retrieved his wallet. The card for Phillips' Home Restoration was tucked behind his license. He punched the number into his cell; after a few rings the call went to voice mail. He hesitated a moment before speaking.

"Hi, Phylicia, this is Jamal Johnson." *You know, the guy you talked to until the sun came up a couple of months ago, and then totally ignored?* "I've got my hands full with this

16

house I'm renovating and could really use your services. Give me a call as soon as possible. Thanks."

Okay, so that hadn't been so hard. Now, all he had to do was survive being around her without succumbing to a death brought on by mind-altering lust.

"Piece of cake," Jamal snorted.

Hunched over a scarred buffet table she'd found at an estate sale a few weeks ago, Phylicia Phillips glided the orbital sander over the wood with painstaking gentleness. She had learned from experience that sacrificing attention to detail in order to save time usually resulted in a piece of unusable material. Phil wasn't sure what she would uncover once she sanded through the layers of paint coating the buffet, but she wasn't willing to compromise the wood in order to find out.

The trill of an old-style rotary telephone wafted from the chest pocket of her denim overalls. Phil set down the sander and pulled out her cell phone. She pushed the plastic face shield up and stared at the unfamiliar number, suppressing the tremors of unease that climbed up her neck whenever she didn't recognize an area code. She'd made an art form out of dodging the bank's phone calls, having memorized their numbers. She figured it was only a matter of time before they sent her name to a collection agency.

Phil waited for voice mail to pick up the call, then sucked in a fortifying breath and dialed into the messaging system. She braced herself for a terse tirade from a collection agency representative, but was startled at the sound of Jamal Johnson's warm, unmistakable voice.

Phil listened to his short message then replayed it, wondering whether there was some twisted mythological fate having a good laugh over this. The only thing that could possibly be worse than a call from a collection agency demanding she catch up on her construction loan payments was a call from Jamal Johnson asking her to help him annihilate her great-great-grandfather's house. The house that had been her family's pride and joy . . . until it had fallen into *her* hands.

A familiar, sickening knot formed in her stomach. If she'd had any idea she would be in danger of losing the Victorian, Phil would never have used it as collateral to fund what had turned out to be the worst business venture *ever*.

It had been a foolproof plan. Purchase

rundown houses for dirt cheap, then flip them for a killer profit. Simple. If only she'd had a crystal ball handy that could have clued her in on the implosion of the housing market.

Phil slumped onto the work stool and cradled her head in her hands.

How had she allowed her life to get to this point?

Oh, wait. Yeah, a man. It was always about a damn man, wasn't it?

Like a fool, she'd let her ex-boyfriend sweet-talk her into partnering with him in the house-flipping venture. Except *she* had been the one who'd taken all the financial risks.

"I hate you, Kevin Winters. I hate you. I hate you. *I hate you.*"

He'd been a pillar of strength when she'd received that first threatening letter from the bank, promising her they would get through the crisis together. That same night, he'd skipped town, taking half of her DVD collection with him. When he'd called from Fresno a week later, Phil had told him she would call the cops and have him arrested for theft if he ever contacted her again. She still wasn't sure if she'd meant it, and hoped to God that man didn't test her by stepping foot back in Gauthier.

She still couldn't believe she'd been so stupid. It was amazing what a normally intelligent woman could be conned into doing for good sex.

Phil massaged her temples. She'd had this argument with herself way too many times over the past year. She wasn't up for it today.

She also wasn't up to working with Jamal Johnson. Ever.

She acknowledged that her aversion to him was wholly unwarranted, and probably a bit irrational, but that didn't change the circumstances. A burst of angry resentment flared up just at the thought of Jamal and his noble contribution to Gauthier's budding tourism industry.

Whatever.

All he'd done was crush her dream of making up for her stupid mistakes. She had been less than five thousand dollars away from securing enough money for the down payment to buy back her family's home when Jamal had decided he wanted to buy it, with some crazy idea of turning it into a bed-and-breakfast.

A bed-and-breakfast, for God's sake!

The thought of countless strangers sleeping in the room her parents once shared made Phil sick to her stomach. For more than a century that house had belonged to the Dufresne family. Her great-great-grandfather had built it with his own two hands. And because of her, a bunch of strange people who probably didn't even care about the home's rich history would now occupy it.

She was not going to help them get there. Jamal would just have to find someone else to work with him.

Recalling the changes he'd made to that gorgeous Georgian he'd bought on Pecan Drive, Phil cringed to think of the Victorian's wonderful interior falling prey to his so-called innovative ideas. That man shouldn't be allowed within a ten-mile radius of a historic structure.

She exhaled a weary, bone-deep sigh, giving herself a few more seconds to wallow in the mess she'd made of this entire situation. Not for the first time, Phil was actually grateful that her mother's dementia-laden brain would prevent her from ever knowing that Phil had lost their family's home.

She swiped at an errant tear and lowered the safety shield back over her face. The more work she got done, the sooner she could get the monkeys off her back. Though now that there was no chance of buying back the Victorian, the motivation to work wasn't as strong.

Phil spent the next hour removing the caked-on paint inch by inch. The rich, caramel-colored oak she unearthed was absolutely breathtaking. Who in their right mind had thought to mask such handsome wood?

Bang! Bang! Bang!

Phil's head popped up. She shut off the sander and pushed the face shield up again as she walked to the side door of her detached garage, which she'd converted into a workshop when she'd bought this house five years ago.

As she swung the door open, a balled fist came barreling forward, straight for her head. It stopped just in time.

"Oh, sorry. Hi." Jamal Johnson stood before her in a pair of khaki deck shorts and a light gray T-shirt. A swath of sweat made a V from his neck to his navel, and dark rings circled under the arms. Apparently, he'd been hard at work . . . ruining her house.

And looking good while doing it. The bastard.

"I hope it's okay that I dropped by," he started. "I was on my way to the hardware store and decided to drive over. Can I come in?" he asked, then moved past her and into the workshop before she could react.

"So, this is the mastermind's laboratory, huh?" he asked, his gaze roaming the shelves she'd custom-built for the countless bottles of varnishes, paint thinners and other materials she used daily. Jamal turned to her. "I left a message on your voice mail. I wasn't sure if you got it."

"I did," she answered stiffly.

His brow peaked. "So, will you be able to help? I really need it. I'm renovating that abandoned Victorian over on Loring Avenue."

It was not abandoned! Phil wanted to yell. Even though no one had lived there since she'd had to put her mother in a special care facility three years ago, Phil had still occasionally checked on the old house. She had *not* abandoned it.

"I realized today that I'm in way over my head," Jamal was saying. "This job is a bit different from the work I did on my house. I gutted most of that one, but I'm trying to preserve the Victorian's woodwork."

His words nearly caused her to slump against the door in relief. Phil had pretty much convinced herself that the next time she drove by the house she'd find rows of solar panels lined up like garden vegetables on the side lawn.

"I apologize for not returning your call,"

23

she said. "But I've been busy today. That's also why I won't be able to help you. I've got several restoration projects lined up," she lied. She had only one small project, to restore a wooden 1931 Crosley antique radio. She had bids on several larger projects at some of the plantation homes in the River Parishes, but not one was guaranteed.

"Tell me you're kidding me," Jamal said with a frustrated groan.

Seeing the anguish on his face, Phil could almost feel sorry for him. As far as she knew, Jamal had no idea that it was her house that he had bought right from under her. But that didn't matter to the irrational part of her brain that thought of him as the enemy.

"I'm sorry," she said again. "But I can't help you."

Still standing next to the door, Phil opened it wider, a clear invitation for him to leave.

He brought a hand up and rubbed the back of his neck. The movement caused his damp T-shirt to stretch across his chest, and Phil found herself in desperate need of ice-cold water.

"Do you at least have a timetable of when you'll be available?" he asked.

"Probably not until the spring," she returned, swatting away the guilt that accompanied the lie. She knew Jamal was on a strict timetable. According to Mya, the bed-and-breakfast was already booked for the entire Christmas in Gauthier celebration, which meant he had three months to finish the house.

"That won't work," he said, his mouth tilting in a frown. "Damn, I guess I'm on my own."

"Guess so," Phil said with false sympathy. She ran another fleeting glance down his body and was once again struck dumb by the picture he created. For a man who had supposedly spent most of his days behind a desk before coming to Gauthier, he had the well-honed body of an athlete. He walked toward her on long, sinewy legs, and the sweat-drenched shirt that clung to his chest and back outlined their chiseled perfection.

Phil had firsthand knowledge of what was hidden underneath the cotton. She recalled how the solid muscles had felt as she'd held on to him during several dances they'd shared at Mya and Corey's wedding reception.

She shook her head, clearing away the untoward thoughts that had no business taking up residence in her head. Hadn't she learned from last year's debacle what a fine-ass man with a pretty smile and nice muscles could lead to? A trip to the poorhouse.

"Good luck on the restoration," Phil said. "It is a restoration that you're performing, right?"

"Yeah, that's what I said."

"No, you said you were *renovating* the house, not restoring it."

"Same thing." He shrugged.

"It absolutely is *not*," Phil stressed. "One means that you're trying to bring it to its former glory; the other often means that you're tearing up the insides and overhauling it with a bunch of modern crap that doesn't belong in there. I just want to know which one you're doing, a restoration or renovation?"

And wasn't she just the epitome of smooth and detached? It wouldn't take much for him to figure out that when it came to the Victorian, she wasn't just an interested bystander.

His curious stare indicated he was halfway to figuring out the puzzle already.

"For the most part it's a restoration," he said.

"Good." She nodded.

"I do plan to make the house eco-friendly, but I need to get the basics done first."

A splotch of red flashed across Phil's

visual field. She should have known this was coming. From the moment she'd walked into the Georgian he'd renovated and saw all of those beautiful cypress floorboards tossed into a pile like so much rubbish, Phil had known this man would wreck any piece of property he got his hands on.

"I need to get back to work," she said through barely clenched teeth.

"So do I. Sorry you can't help. I could really use your expertise."

Phil couldn't form the words to respond. She knew if she opened her mouth she would regret it. Instead, she nodded and closed the door behind him. Moments later, she heard an ignition turn over and his truck drive away. On shaky legs she walked back to the buffet she'd been restoring. She placed the safety shield back over her eyes and picked up the sander. She didn't even try to wipe away the tears that trailed down her cheeks.

CHAPTER 2

Jamal tossed a pack of screw anchors into his shopping basket and headed for the lighting aisle. He'd accidentally cracked the bulb in his hanging work lamp, which had forced him to stop working once the sun went down. He couldn't afford to work only during daylight hours anymore, not if Belle Maison was going to open as scheduled.

Maybe he could run a special promotion: get half off your stay if you're willing to pick up a hammer.

"Get a grip," Jamal said under his breath.

He had contractors lined up to do most of the big-ticket items — to paint the exterior and strip and refinish the home's original hardwood flooring. What he needed was someone with expertise in restoring some of the home's unique elements that he wanted to preserve.

Jamal was having a hard time deciding whether he was upset or relieved that Phylicia was too busy to help. He could use her skill with a detailing chisel, but he sure as hell had not been looking forward to the cold showers that were undoubtedly in his future if he had to spend any significant time working alongside her.

It didn't matter now, did it?

Corey had warned him that Phylicia's skills were a hot commodity. He should have known her calendar was booked months in advance.

Jamal grabbed a replacement halogen lamp and frowned at the rows of pear-shaped incandescent bulbs stacked on the shelves. He shook his head. Were people really still using those things?

He made his way to the hardware store's single checkout counter, where a group of older men were loitering. After several trips here, Jamal had discovered that the three men who lingered around the counter were not customers but retirees who spent much of their day shooting the breeze with Nathan Robottom.

"Hey, it's the architect," Nathan greeted.

"Hello, Mr. Robottom. Gentlemen." Jamal nodded to the group as he placed his items on the counter.

"How's the work coming on the new hotel?" Nathan asked.

"Not a hotel, just a bed-and-breakfast," Jamal corrected him. "And it's coming along just fine."

"You think it'll be done in time for the Christmas in Gauthier celebration?" a man Jamal knew only as Froggy asked in a gravelly, toadlike voice. Hence the nickname, Jamal assumed. "My granddaughter lives up in Michigan. Said she saw an advertisement for Gauthier's Christmas celebration on the internet all the way up there."

"It's the same internet wherever you are," Nathan said with an eye roll. "Why do you think they call it the *World Wide* Web?"

"Well, hell, I don't fool with that internet," Froggy blustered.

Jamal suppressed the urge to laugh. "Mya Dubois-Anderson is in charge of publicizing it, so I have no doubt word of Christmas in Gauthier will reach far and wide."

"Gauthier owes you a lot for opening this hotel," Nathan said. "It's nice to have tourists passing through, but it will be even better when they can stay for a couple of days and spend some money."

Jamal nodded. He knew just how much having Belle Maison up and running would mean for Gauthier's local economy.

"I was hoping you gentlemen could suggest someone who could help me with the renovations. I've got a few guys coming out to do the heavy lifting, but I need someone who can handle the delicate woodworking without damaging it."

"Did you try Phi—" Froggy started.

"I just came from Phylicia Phillips's place," Jamal said, cutting him off. "She's booked up."

"Yeah, Phil gets a lot of work. Did you see the job she did on the Rosedale Plantation?" Nathan whistled. "That girl is better with a wood chisel than her daddy was."

"Do you know of anyone else?" Jamal asked. He didn't particularly want to hear about how good Phylicia would have been. Dammit, he *knew* how good she would have been. Maybe if he offered her twice whatever the job she was currently working on paid? Would she consider giving it up and coming to work for him?

Jamal winced at the selfish thought. He didn't know much about Phylicia, but she didn't seem like someone who would risk damaging her reputation for a few extra bucks. If anyone could respect the notion of integrity and a strong work ethic over money, it was him. He could be making an impressive salary as an architect with his family's construction business, instead of reallocating money from his savings in order to open a bed-and-breakfast. But he was a helluva lot happier, and no amount of money was worth giving that up.

"If you think of someone else who may be able to help, give me a call," Jamal told Nathan as he pocketed his change and headed out of the hardware store.

He waved at a couple of folks as he drove down Gauthier's Main Street. For a city kid, he'd allowed this small town to thoroughly charm him. It looked like something out of a Norman Rockwell painting, with its brightly colored storefronts sporting striped awnings and hand-painted We're Open signs hanging in the windows. Jamal hadn't known towns like this still existed, especially with predominately black populations.

Moving to Gauthier had been, without a doubt, one of the best decisions he'd made in his thirty-three years. He had been slowly dying back in Phoenix, but this small town had given him a new start. Having the freedom to live life on his terms instead of being bound by the confines of the Johnson Construction legacy had changed everything. He was finally free to pursue his dreams of opening his own architectural firm, without having to face his father's derision.

So why was his firm still just an idea on paper?

A jolt of anxiety ricocheted against the walls of Jamal's chest. The sensation had become commonplace, rearing its head whenever his mind so much as tiptoed in the vicinity of his underdeveloped career plans.

He quieted the unease by picturing the Victorian and what it would mean to Gauthier. The men back at the hardware store had reiterated how appreciative the town was that he was renovating Belle Maison. It would be selfish to think about his architectural firm when so many would benefit from the B&B.

"Yeah, you're all about the noble self-sacrifice," Jamal muttered.

Renovating the Victorian was a stalling tactic, and he damn well knew it. Just like the renovations of the Georgian he'd purchased when he moved to Gauthier a year ago.

He didn't have the time or energy for a mental debate over why he continued to avoid moving forward on his architectural firm. There was too much work to be done, regardless of the true reason he was doing it.

Despite his exhaustion, Jamal drove

straight past his house, forfeiting the hot shower and food his body craved in exchange for getting in a few more hours of work on Belle Maison. Now that he had the replacement bulb for his work light, there was no reason for him to call it quits for the day.

Sitting at the bar in her kitchen after a fitful night of very little sleep, Phil sipped a cup of piping-hot coffee and thumbed through the latest issue of *Antique Abodes*. There was a feature on a Greek Revival in Natchez, Mississippi, that a young couple had spent the past five years restoring. She wondered if she could swing a trip up to Natchez. It was worth the three-hour drive to see the house firsthand.

If she was lucky, she wouldn't have the time to drive into Mississippi to look at someone else's restoration project; she would be too busy with her own. The caretaker at Evergreen Plantation had emailed yesterday afternoon, informing Phil that a decision would be made soon on the restoration job she'd bid on. It wasn't a huge project — a bit of work on some of the plantation's antique furniture — but it would be welcomed income. She was barely keeping her head above water, and the waterline was gradually creeping further up her neck.

Phil spotted the mail carrier in front of her next-door neighbor's house. She set her coffee cup down and was waiting outside when Paul Ricard pulled up to her mailbox.

"How you doing, Phil?" he greeted.

"Doing okay," she answered. "How's Liza? Baby Number Five make an appearance yet?"

"Any day now," Paul said, handing her a stack of envelopes and catalogs. "Liza's at that stage when she's not talking to me. That usually means we're close to a delivery."

"Well, if she still hasn't figured out what to call the new baby, I think Phylicia is a beautiful name."

"That it is." Paul laughed. "See you later, Phil."

She waved as she turned and headed back toward the house, thumbing through the mail. There were two credit card offers — her current financial state must not have reached those companies yet — the bill for her auto insurance and an advertisement for the grand opening of a dry cleaners in Maplesville.

The fifth envelope caused her heart to sputter and her breathing to escalate. Phil stared at the return address, dread suffusing her bones. A weight settled in her stomach as she reentered the house and went into the kitchen. Stalling, she tossed the mail on the bar and refilled her coffee cup.

Leaning a hip against the counter, Phil eyed the envelope from Mossy Oaks Care Facility. She already knew what it contained. She'd received an envelope just like it about a month ago, with a letter stating that the rising cost of health care was forcing the facility to increase its rates across the board. Even with the money from her dad's life insurance policy, Phil was still paying nearly a thousand dollars out of her own pocket every month for her mother's care. She couldn't afford several hundred more.

But she couldn't afford not to pay it, either.

It was nothing short of a miracle that one of the South's most renowned care facilities for dementia patients was located just twenty miles southeast, in Slidell. It was ludicrous to even consider moving her mom from Mossy Oaks.

Phil swallowed the lump of worry that lodged in her throat as she set the cup on the counter and reached for the envelope. She opened it, finding exactly what she knew would be there. The increase had been approved by the facility's board of directors and would take effect next month.

Where was she going to find this money?

Her cell phone trilled. Phil picked it up and recognized the number from Evergreen Plantation's caretaker. She glanced up at the ceiling and whispered, "Thank you, Lord," as she answered it.

But instead of answered prayers, Phil had her heart broken into bite-size chunks. The caretaker's apologetic tone was nearly as hard to stomach as the words she spoke.

"I'm sorry, Miss Phillips, but Marshall Restoration's bid was significantly less than yours, even with the cost of shipping the furniture to their California warehouse."

"But aren't you afraid the furniture will get damaged in transit?" Phil asked.

"The furniture is insured," was the woman's response.

As if that mattered!

It wasn't about the money, Phil wanted to shout. It was about potentially endangering irreplaceable, centuries-old furniture. There shouldn't be a price tag on that. But apparently there was, and it was lower than the eight thousand dollars Phil had bid on the work.

Before ending the call she asked that she be kept in mind for other work the plantation might need in the future. Phil slouched over the bar, her head landing with a thump on her forearm. The disappointment was almost too much to bear.

As much as she loved her work, Phil wished she could count on a steady paycheck. When she did get paid it was usually enough to live on for several months, depending on the size of the job. But her last big project had been back in the spring, and repairing an old radio or the occasional antique headboard was not going to cut it. She needed a long-term project, something that would provide enough income to last her until one of the other bids hopefully came through.

She knew of one job that would fit the bill, but Lord knew she did not want to take it.

"No, no, *no,*" she whispered, her whine muffled by her arm.

There had to be another option.

Phil glanced toward the hallway, thinking of the Hepplewhite furniture in her guest bedroom. The set had been passed down in her family for generations. Phil knew if she had it appraised by one of the antique dealers in New Orleans it would fetch a hefty sum, but after losing Belle Maison she couldn't stomach parting with the few pieces of furniture she'd managed to retain.

With her mother's mind slowly slipping away, they were the only ties she had left to her past.

"Oh, God," Phil moaned. She would have to accept Jamal's job offer. She was in no position to turn down work.

She pushed herself up and drained the rest of the coffee from her mug. If it were not still midmorning she would have been tempted to refill the mug with whiskey. But alcohol wouldn't solve anything. She'd allowed herself to fall into this hole. She would have to be the one to claw herself out.

Phil quickly changed into a pair of jeans. In her never-ending quest to hold fast to her femininity, she donned a pair of tiny butterfly-shaped earrings before scooping her hair into a ponytail. Filling her dad's old thermos with the remaining coffee, she grabbed her keys and headed out the door.

Fingers of dread crept further up her spine with every mile her tires ate up on the road. By the time she arrived at the stately yellow-and-white Victorian where she grew up, Phil was on the verge of losing her breakfast.

This was going to be torture. Plain and simple.

No, not simple. There was nothing simple about this. It was tragic, an ironic twist of fate that would torment her for years to come. It was bad enough that it was due to her mistakes that the home no longer belonged to her family. The fact that she would now play a part in its ruination sickened her to no end.

"Nothing you can do about it now," she muttered.

She pulled in behind a jet-black double-cab Ford F-150. Phil couldn't help but admire the truck's chrome package; the tire rims and front grille gleamed. That had probably set him back a few thousand dollars, she thought with a disgusted snort.

She knew architects did pretty well, but Phil also knew that Jamal's seemingly endless flow of cash did not come solely from his profession. According to Mya, Jamal had a trust fund the size of the Louisiana Superdome, and his family owned one of the largest construction firms in Arizona.

The fact that he was a millionaire without a financial care in the world made this even worse. She'd been struggling just to raise the capital for the down payment on this house. He'd probably bought the Victorian outright with cash from his rainy day fund.

Phil stifled her irritation as she walked along the brick-laid walkway that led to the huge wraparound porch. Her heart broke a bit more with every step she took. She trudged up the porch steps, fingering the balustrade. It needed sanding and a new coat of paint. She should have taken care of this months ago, even if the house had belonged to the bank at the time.

"Phylicia?"

Phil turned with a start. Jamal approached her, wiping his hands on a tattered rag. He was dressed in shorts and another of those sweat-stained T-shirts that clung to his washboard abs.

Oh, yeah. This would be torture.

Phil pulled in a deep breath and let it out slowly, willing her eyes to concentrate on his face and not his six-pack.

Of course, his face could get her in just as much trouble as the rest of his body. His skin was smooth and light brown, his eyes a darker brown, but with flecks of gold. Phil remembered being stunned when she'd noticed the sparkling flecks as they danced at Corey and Mya's wedding reception. Those eyes were framed by thick, beautiful lashes that any woman would envy, yet they didn't detract from his masculinity one bit. They made his eyes richer, more seductive.

An embarrassingly swift shudder of need shot through her.

Not this guy, she told her hyperaware

41

libido. There were other eligible men in Gauthier. She would not allow herself to lust after the one who'd bought her family's home out from under her.

Well, she wouldn't lust after him more than she did already.

"Can I help you with something?" Jamal asked.

"Actually, I'm here to help you," Phil answered, pushing thoughts of his eyes, abs and everything else out of her mind. "One of the projects I thought I would be working on fell through. It freed up space on my calendar."

His relieved grin transformed his face into a thing of even greater beauty, if that were possible.

"You have no idea how happy I am to hear that." Jamal stuffed the rag into his back pocket. "Well, I guess a tour is in order. Let me show you around the property."

"Oh, you don't have —" Phil started to tell him she probably knew this house better than he did, but she stopped herself. What if his Realtor had shared that the home he'd purchased had been repossessed by the bank because the previous owner had defaulted on the loan? Did she really want Jamal knowing that much about her personal business? No, thank you.

"Sure," Phil said with false brightness. "I can't wait to see it."

CHAPTER 3

As they entered the vestibule, Phil tried to hold back the wistful smiles that threatened as dozens of bittersweet memories sprouted to mind. When she was younger, she'd had an army of imaginary friends whom she would play hide-and-seek with throughout the massive house. She even let them win sometimes.

When she got older, she and Mya would have slumber parties. Using a special scale they had devised, they would rate the boys at school. Corey Anderson, who eventually became Mya's boyfriend, and finally, after fifteen years apart, her husband, always scored the top rating.

Phil glanced over at Jamal. He would have given Corey a run for his money back in the day.

"This is what sold me on the house," Jamal said, running his palm along the ornately carved banister that traveled up

44

the staircase. "Look at this detailing. The Realtor said it was all done by hand."

"It's beautiful," Phil remarked. When she was eight years old, she had broken her arm sliding down that very same banister after seeing it done in a movie. As much of a tomboy as she'd been back then, it was a wonder she'd made it through the rest of her childhood without any more broken bones.

"Why don't we start upstairs?" Jamal said. "There's less work needed up there. We can take a quick look around before discussing the really intense stuff."

She followed him up the stairs, gawking unabashedly at the way the shorts fit over his butt. It was too damn firm. *He* was too damn *fine.*

Lethal. That's the rating Jamal would have received on the scale she'd developed with Mya all those years ago. His smile, his naturally wavy hair, those sinewy muscles, his scent — clean, yet spicy. Everything about him was lethal, especially to a woman who had gone over a year without a man in her bed. Her battery-operated toys were fine for providing temporary relief, but she couldn't snuggle up to a vibrator. She missed snuggling. She missed men.

But she sure as hell didn't miss the heartache they caused.

That's what she would remember when she caught a glimpse of Jamal's gold-speckled eyes and charming smile. Kevin had nice eyes and a sexy smile, too.

"There are three bedrooms and another small room in the rear that the Realtor said was used as a sitting room, but I'm going to turn it into an additional bedroom. The biggest problem is there's only one bathroom up here, which means if the B&B is at full capacity, I'll have eight adults sharing one bathroom."

"That can pose a problem," Phil said. "I can only imagine what it would be like if you have a bunch of women staying here for a girls' weekend."

"World War Three." Jamal chuckled.

Dammit, even his laugh was sexy. Accepting this job was *such* a bad idea.

"After growing up in a house with my mother and younger sister, I know what it's like to fight over the bathroom," he continued.

Phil twisted around to look at him. "You had to fight for bathroom time in the house you grew up in? I thought your family owned half of Phoenix?"

"My family doesn't own half of Phoenix," he said, then his smile took on a chastised

46

quality. "Okay, so the fights for the bath-room happened at the beach house in Malibu."

Malibu? Is he for real?

Phil managed to resist a well-deserved eye roll, but she couldn't tamp down the bitter resentment that climbed up her throat. Jamal Johnson would never know how it felt to sweat over making next month's mort-gage payment.

He gestured with his head for her to fol-low him. "C'mon. We'll discuss some of the ideas I have in mind for the house."

As they made their way back down the stairs, Phil ran her fingers along the silk wall coverings.

Jamal glanced over his shoulder. "Beauti-ful, isn't it? Everything in this house is great. I'm lucky it was still on the market."

"Yeah," Phil said, hoping the emotion that instantly filled her throat didn't come through her voice. "I'm surprised Belle Mai-son stayed on the market for as long as it did." And heartbroken that it hadn't re-mained there just a little while longer.

"The house was in pretty good shape. I have a work crew coming in to give it a new paint job, both inside and out, and to take care of a couple of other details, but they can't start for another four weeks. In the meantime, I've been working on a few things that needed to be addressed right away, like the cracks in the dining room wall."

"The walls were cracked in the dining room?" Phil asked, unable to conceal the astonishment in her voice. When had that happened? She'd checked on this house at least once a month.

But then Phil remembered that her last few check-ins had consisted of a quick drive-by and cursory look from her truck's driver's side window. Too much work to do, and all that. The excuses had flowed like a waterfall, sounding good enough to her ears.

But as she took in the musty smell from the house being closed up for so long and noticed the dust that had accumulated on the walls and baseboards, the picture became clearer. And the shame it caused nearly suffocated her.

From the moment she'd moved her mom into Mossy Oaks, Phil had started to neglect this house, seeing it more as a burden than a part of her history. It took losing it to appreciate what she'd had.

Phil followed Jamal into the formal dining room. And stopped cold.

"Drywall?" she said. "You're putting up *drywall*?"

"Only one section of the wall was cracked, but I figured I'd just redo the entire room."

"With *drywall*?"

He measured her with a curious stare. "What do you have against drywall?"

"You mean besides the fact that it has no business in an 1870s Victorian? It also greatly reduces the resale value of the house."

He waved off her concern. "I'm not concerned about resale value right now."

This is no longer my house, she reminded herself. Jamal owned it; he could do whatever he wanted with it. Even if it meant putting up freaking drywall.

"Just . . . show me the rest," she said.

"Here's one of the things I'm putting into your capable hands," he said, pointing to the pocket doors that recessed into the walls between the dining room and kitchen. "They're pretty banged up, but if at all possible, I want to keep them."

"Of course you want to keep them. They add too much character to this house to think of getting rid of them."

Phil glided her hand along the smooth mud where the panels of Sheetrock met. She could not believe the man was replacing the classic plaster walls with drywall, but at least he'd done a good job.

"You did this work by yourself?" she asked.

Jamal nodded. "Have I impressed the guru?"

"Stop calling me that."

"Why not? Everyone else does."

"First, I'm not a guru," Phil sad. "My dad deserved that title, not me. And secondly, I work mostly in wood and wrought iron, so I'm not the one to properly judge drywall installation."

"That's too bad," he said. "I was hoping you'd be impressed."

Phil looked over at him and was caught off guard by the sexy smile pulling at the edge of his lips. She knew flirting when she saw it, and she was definitely seeing it in action right now.

That would *not* be good. She could not handle a sweaty, sexy, flirting Jamal Johnson.

"So, besides the doors, what else is there?" she asked.

"I've got my blueprints out here," he said, motioning for her to follow him outside.

Phil stopped short. "If you're not doing a renovation, why did you draw up blueprints for a house that's already built?"

He shrugged. "You work in wood and wrought iron, I work in blueprints. It just makes it easier to have a map of the house so I can pinpoint each thing that needs to be addressed."

She accepted his explanation with the same amount of guarded skepticism in which she took everything else he told her. Outside, the blueprints were spread out on the top of a folding table, held at each corner with pieces of leftover wood. She stood next to Jamal as he pointed out various jobs that needed to be done throughout the house. She tried to ignore the combination of sweat, sawdust and man that flooded her senses. Ignoring a ten-piece brass band blowing in her ear would have been easier.

"My biggest headache right now is fixtures," Jamal was saying. "I'd love to get something comparable to what's in the downstairs bathroom and kitchen, but I can't find anything even close."

Phil ordered herself to focus on the job at hand, and not on his scent. Or the muscles rippling underneath his T-shirt. Or the way she'd clung to them when they'd danced months ago.

"You won't find them in hardware stores," Phil said. "Your best bet will be companies that specialize in reclaimed fixtures. They salvage pieces and sell them to people restoring older properties. I've got several contacts I can check for you."

When he didn't comment for several moments, Phil glanced over at him. That smile was back, the one that made her heart beat just a bit quicker.

"I knew I'd come to the right person," he said. "Together we're going to take Belle Maison in a completely new direction."

Yeah, that's what she was afraid of.

As Phylicia leaned over the table, studying the blueprints, Jamal studied *her*. He couldn't get over just how much of a contradiction she was. She worked in a decidedly male-dominated field, yet those high cheekbones, amazingly deep brown eyes and lush, full lips could easily grace the cover of a fashion magazine.

She was tall and slim, but years of manual labor had added definition to her arms and shoulders. Jamal remembered how they had looked in the sleeveless bridesmaid gown she'd worn at the wedding.

Why had someone so sexy, so feminine, decided to work with hammers and sanders? Probably because she was damn good at it. He'd noticed several pieces of furniture in various stages of restoration when he'd visited her workshop yesterday. She seemed to spend most of her time laboring over stuff most people would write off as useless.

But in her hands, what was once decrepit gained new life.

She tilted her head to the side and her ponytail draped along her neck. Jamal had the strongest urge to run his fingers through it, lift it off her neck and taste the skin underneath. It would probably get him slapped.

Yet, if he'd done the same thing the night of the wedding, Jamal was certain his kiss would not only have been welcome, but reciprocated. He didn't understand what had gone wrong. Unless . . .

"Are you seeing someone?"

Phylicia's head popped up, her stunned eyes widening. "Excuse me?"

Okay, so maybe he could have been a tad more subtle. But he didn't do subtle all that well, and he wasn't in the mood for playing games.

"Are you in a relationship?" he asked. "Is that why you avoided my calls after Corey and Mya's wedding?"

"No, I don't have a boyfriend. But —"

"Good," he said.

"No, not good," she returned. "It's none of your business."

Jamal crossed his arms over his chest and challenged her with a direct stare.

"Don't do this, Phylicia. Don't pretend

you didn't feel that spark between us at Mya and Corey's wedding. We were together the entire night."

"I was the maid of honor and you were the best man," she said. "Of course we spent a lot of time in each other's company at the reception. But we were not *together* together."

"What about after the reception? The sun was coming up by the time I brought you home. We talked for hours that night, Phylicia, yet when I called you the next day, it was as if you didn't know who I was."

"Jamal, please." She put her hands up. "I'm not looking to get involved with anyone, even on a casual basis. If you want me to work with you on the restoration, know that it is the *only* thing I'm willing to undertake. I don't mix business with my personal life. Now, what exactly are you looking for from me?"

He cocked his head to the side. "Let me get this straight. Are you saying that if I choose to see you on a personal level, you wouldn't help me with the house?"

"Actually, you don't have a choice. The two of us getting involved is not an option."

"Why the hell not?"

"Because I said so. Now, are we going to go over these plans, or am I getting in my truck and going home?" The sharp edge to her voice brooked no further argument.

Jamal glanced at the pile of construction debris just over her shoulder, trying like hell to rein in the frustration that threatened to topple him. He was itching to make her admit that what he'd felt that night had not been one-sided. Pulling her close and kissing the hell out of her would accomplish that.

It would also guarantee that she would leave the property and likely never come back. And that was *not* an option.

"Blueprints," Jamal bit out.

Phylicia bobbed a curt nod and leaned over the blueprints. Jamal studied her with a mixture of frustration and disappointment — heavy on the disappointment. Catching a whiff of the soft, flowery scent that drifted from her hair only made things worse.

She pointed to the materials list. "Exactly what is strawboard, and why do you need so much of it?"

"It's a building material made from compressed wheat and rice straw," he answered. "I'm redoing the upstairs bedrooms with it."

Her eyes rolled. "This is another of your environmentally friendly things, isn't it?"

"Yes, it's considered green technology,"

Jamal replied with a defensive edge he'd tried, but failed, to keep from his tone. "Strawboard is as durable as plaster and drywall and more fire- and mold-resistant than either of the other materials. It also provides better sound insulation, so guests won't be disturbed by what may be going on in the next room."

"But what about the wainscoting in the bedrooms? It's over a hundred years old," Phylicia protested.

"I'm not getting rid of the wainscoting."

"But you can damage it by removing it. And if you think bathroom fixtures are hard to find, just try century-old beadboard wainscoting."

"That's why you're here," he said. "To make sure none of this valuable original woodworking gets damaged."

She brought both hands up and rubbed her temples. Jamal was pretty sure she wanted to strangle him.

"What's this?" she asked, pointing at a spot he'd X-ed out on the blueprint.

"It's an odd little room on the other side of the house. Looks as if it was added long after the original structure was built."

"I know about the room," she said. "What are you planning to do with it?"

"Get rid of it."

Her brows spiked in shock. "Why?" she asked with enough distress to give him pause.

"Because it sticks out like a sore thumb," Jamal answered cautiously. "I want the house to be as authentic as possible, and the room takes away from the original design."

"Authentic!" she screeched. "You're putting strawboard walls in a Queen Anne Victorian, yet you're claiming you want authenticity?" Her expression darkened, those smoky brown eyes turning almost black. "Of all people, I cannot believe this house fell into *your* hands."

"What the hell is that supposed to mean?"

"You are going to destroy it!"

"The house was abandoned," Jamal pointed out. "It was already on its way to being ruined."

"It was *not* abandoned!" she shouted. "I'm sick and tired of everyone saying the house was frigging abandoned!" She slapped her hands on the table. "I can't do this."

The emotion he heard clogging her voice shot a lightning rod of alarm through him. "Phylicia, what's going on here?" he asked.

"I'm sorry." She pulled in a deep breath. "You'll have to find someone else to help you."

She glanced up at him for the briefest moment, but it was long enough for Jamal to notice the sheen in her eyes. He caught her by the elbow, but she jerked away from him and half walked, half ran to her truck.

"Phylicia!" Jamal called, but her truck was already backing out of the driveway. Jamal stood in complete shock, trying to figure out just what in the hell he'd done wrong this time.

CHAPTER 4

Phil pulled into her driveway and hopped out of her truck, making a beeline for her workshop. She needed a solid hour of mind-numbing work before she could even think about doing anything else. She wanted to hit something with her mallet. Hard. But she'd passed the pounding stage on all of the projects she currently had in the works.

The blowtorch would have to do.

Phil headed for the back of the shop. She lowered the safety shield over her face and ignited the blowtorch. Moments later, she was lost in the piece she had been working on for the past few months.

With painstaking precision she carved intricate loops and curlicues through the metal she'd found at a scrapyard, creating a lace effect. Immediately, the lace curtains that once hung in her mother's painting room popped into her mind, and her hand slipped.

"Dammit," Phil cursed. She released the trigger on the blowtorch and surveyed the damage her slip had caused to the metal. Nothing too noticeable, thank goodness.

"Phylicia?"

Phil nearly fell off the stool at the unexpected summons. She whipped around, the blowtorch still in her hand.

Jamal took two giant steps back, his hands raised in surrender. "Careful with that."

Phil lifted the safety shield from her face but didn't put down the blowtorch. "How did you get in here?"

"The door wasn't locked."

Of course it wasn't. She lived in Gauthier. She never locked the door to her shop while she was working. She'd have to rethink that. This was the second time he had crept up on her.

"What do you want?" she asked.

"I want to know what happened back at the house," he said. "Why did you run off?"

Phil's entire being sagged in defeat. It was no use withholding the truth from him. He would eventually find out. With the way gossip traveled in this small town, she was surprised no one had revealed Belle Maison's previous owner to him already.

"It's my house," Phil said. His confused expression would have been comical if there was anything even remotely funny about any of this. "The Victorian that you have all these fancy plans for? It's my family's home. It's where I grew up."

"But the bank said they owned —"

"Yes, the bank owned it," she cut him off. "It's a very long story that I'm not about to get into, especially with you."

"What's that supposed to mean? *Especially with me?* When did I become the bad guy, Phylicia?"

"When you bought my family's home and decided to make it into a bed-and-breakfast." Phil raised her palm, stanching his protest. "This isn't your fault, and I know you don't deserve any of the disgust I feel toward you."

He flinched at her harsh word choice, and Phil felt even worse.

"I'm sorry. That was uncalled for," she said. Phil shook her head. "I just can't do this, Jamal. What you're doing? Opening this B&B? It's a great thing for Gauthier. It's going to be a huge draw for tourists, and I know the businesses on Main Street are going to benefit from it. But that's my house," she said, pointing east toward Belle Maison. "It's hard to see it being destroyed."

"I'm not going to destroy the house. How many times do I have to say that?"

"When it comes to this sort of thing, it seems we have different definitions of what it means to destroy. And you *are* planning to destroy a part of the house."

"Just that one room," he said.

"It's the most important room in the house!" Phil yelled.

She covered her face with her hands and pulled in a deep breath. As the tears collected in her throat, Phil mentally cursed each and every one of them. But it was too hard to maintain a stoic facade. She was never one for wearing her heart on her sleeve, but when it came to her mother, she couldn't hold back.

Phil bit her lower lip to help curb the wavering. She wiped at the tears that traveled down her cheeks.

"Twenty years ago, my father built that room for my mother. It's where she painted. She needed a place with plenty of natural sunlight, and there wasn't a room on the east side of the house that was suitable. She would spend hours in that room. Her painting meant everything to her."

Phil sucked in a deep breath. "I've lost so much of her already. Hearing that you planned to tear down her room . . . It was just too much."

She couldn't interpret the expression on

Jamal's face. He just stood there, staring at her, and her discomfort grew with every nanosecond that passed.

"I'm sorry," he finally said. "I had no idea. About any of it. The bank never told me anything about the previous owner. Shit, Corey didn't even say anything."

"I was surprised neither Corey nor Mya told you it was my family home. But neither of them knows how Belle Maison ended up on the market. Mya believes I put it up for sale intentionally." She looked up at him. "I never would have let the property go if I'd had a choice. I love that house. It's been in my family for generations."

His mouth dipped in a frown. "Phylicia, I'm really sorry that you had to sell your family's home, but I've invested too much into this project not to see it through."

"Oh, God, I'm not asking you not to go forth with the B&B. I'm a businesswoman, Jamal. I understand how these things work. You bought the house. It's yours. I just can't be a part of the restoration process. I thought I could, but to stand there and watch my mother's room being torn to the ground?" Phil shook her head. "I just can't do it."

Several moments passed before Jamal asked in a gentle voice, "What if I don't touch that room?"

Phil's eyes shot to his. She didn't want to believe the sincerity she saw there. "You would do that?"

He took a step toward her. "The room isn't hurting anybody," he said.

His deep brown eyes searched her face. When he reached toward her, Phil stiffened, but he only captured the safety shield and pulled it off her head.

"Besides," he continued, "as you pointed out, I'm making a lot of other changes, so my authenticity argument doesn't carry much weight. And the house holds senti-mental value for you."

"For *me*, not you."

"It's clear how much it would hurt if the room was destroyed. I don't want to be the one who hurts you, Phylicia." He reached forward and lifted her ponytail from where it draped along her neck. "I think someone did that already."

She gazed at him, feeling as if she'd been drawn into a trance by his hushed voice. "Why do you always call me Phylicia?"

The edge of his mouth quirked in a smile. "Because it's your name."

"Everyone else calls me Phil."

"That's a man's name. And despite that blowtorch you were wielding a few minutes ago, there's no denying that you are all woman, Phylicia."

As he dipped his head toward her, a tiny voice told Phil to move out of his reach. But a much louder voice told her to stay right where she was. It had been way too long since she'd been kissed, and after the day she'd had, Phil couldn't think of a single thing she needed more.

The moment Jamal's soft lips touched hers her heart melted. He was gentle in his coaxing, but insistent, his lips enticing her to join in. He cupped the back of her head and slanted his to the side to get a better angle.

Phil heard a moan but couldn't tell which one of them had made the sound. Without fully recognizing what she was doing, she linked her hands behind Jamal's neck and cradled the back of his head. She parted her lips and thrust her tongue inside his mouth, losing herself in the kiss.

An animalistic growl rose from his throat. Jamal held her in place as his tongue plunged into her mouth. He tasted like cinnamon, spicy and sweet, and as his tongue made itself at home in her mouth, Phil allowed herself to enjoy it. He knew just what to do, applying just the right amount of pressure before pulling slightly away, making her reach for him.

After she had enough fodder to fill her nightly fantasies for a while, Phil ended the kiss, leaving Jamal with a dazed expression, his eyes heavy with desire.

She took several steps back. "Did you offer to leave the room untouched just so you could get away with kissing me?" Phil asked, trying to add some levity to the sexually charged tension suffusing the room.

"No," he said, a hint of humor tingeing his voice. "I promised not to touch the room because it's the right thing to do, but I would have kissed you anyway," he said. "I've been dying to kiss you since Mya and Corey's wedding. And that was before I saw you holding a blowtorch. That just pushed me over the edge."

Phil rolled her eyes. Despite the fireworks his kiss had set off within her, she needed to reiterate her previous assertion. "I meant what I said, Jamal. If we're going to work together, you can't do that again."

"What? Kiss you?"

She nodded.

He blew out a ragged breath. "Are you really going to make me choose between kissing you and having you work on the house? That's not fair."

"Wait a minute. Didn't we already have

this conversation?" Phil asked. "There is no choice. The whole you-and-me thing isn't going to happen."

"Come on, Phylicia. You know we'd be good together."

"I don't know any such thing," she returned.

A simple, sexy brow quirked. "Need me to show you again?"

Phil's insides quaked with instant want. God, this man was dangerous to her undersexed body.

She picked up the blowtorch. "Stay back. I mean it."

Jamal's head pitched back with a crack of laughter. "You definitely have a dangerous side to you, Phylicia Phillips." He leaned in close and whispered in her ear, "You should know that I like that in a woman." He winked at her, then turned and headed for the door. "I'll see you at Belle Maison tomorrow morning," Jamal called over his shoulder.

She watched him walk out of her workshop, and a part of her wanted to follow him. How was she going to survive the next couple of months working alongside that man? Especially now that she knew how he tasted.

As she tapped the igniter on the burner

head and connected the blue flame with the metal, Phil muttered, "Boy, you just love heaping trouble on your head, don't you?"

CHAPTER 5

"Good morning."

Jamal looked up from the board he was measuring. He couldn't contain his smile as Phylicia walked toward him, carrying a thermos. He was constantly amazed at the way this woman could make faded jeans and a plain white T-shirt look sexy.

"Good morning," he returned.

She took a healthy sip from her thermos before capping it and allowed her eyes to roam around the yard. Finally, she looked his way, giving him her full attention, and the current that zapped between them was enough to singe the hair on his skin.

Phylicia cleared her throat. "I thought about your plans on how to tackle the restoration," she began. "I think you may be setting yourself up for more work if you go one room at a time. You should just tear down everything at once."

Her all-business tone made it apparent

that she had no plans to pick up where they'd left off after yesterday's kiss.

Jamal folded his arms across his chest, one brow cocked. *So that's how it's going to be?*

Phylicia lifted her chin. *Damn right.*

His mind recoiled in protest, but Jamal knew it was for the best, especially with all the work that needed to be done and the limited time he had left before guests began arriving. But there were *after*-work hours. And the work crew he'd hired would soon add a lot more manpower to the project.

"Are you ready to get to it?" Phylicia asked, all business. "I could get started on removing the wainscoting today."

"I thought you wanted me to leave the wainscoting untouched?" he asked.

"It's your house, Jamal." She scrunched up her nose. "You have no idea how hard it was for me to say that."

"Phyl—" he started, but she put her hand up, halting him.

"It is *your* house. You agreed to leave my mom's painting room intact, which I am unbelievably grateful for, but I don't expect you to change all of your plans just to suit me. You hired me to help preserve elements of Belle Maison's original structure; that's what I'm here to do."

"I also hired you for your input," he said.

"I'm open to suggestions. Doesn't mean I'll go along with all of them, but as highly recommended as you come, I'd be a fool not to listen to what you have to say."

He tossed the measuring tape aside and moved toward her. "I want us to work together as a team."

He reached for her, but she took several steps back. She held her hands up, her face resolute. "Look, Jamal, I already told you that if I'm going to work with you on this project, what happened yesterday afternoon cannot happen again. That kiss was . . . well, it was a mistake."

"It wasn't a mistake," he disputed. "It was unbelievable."

"Jamal —"

"Don't shut me down without at least giving me a chance, Phylicia."

"It's not going to happen," she reiterated. "I have too much going on in my life right now. And with you and this house and just . . . It's not going to happen. Is that going to be a problem for you?"

He raised his palms up, giving her the universal hands-off gesture. What he really wanted to do was kiss the living daylights out of her again. Apparently, she'd quickly forgotten how explosive their kiss was yesterday. He, on the other hand, couldn't

71

get it out of his head.

"Good," she said with a curt nod. "I'll get to work on the parlor."

Arms crossed over his chest, Jamal stepped to the side so she could move past him. As he watched her walk up the back steps and into the house, he couldn't imagine how he would get through the next few months working alongside her.

As it turned out, he didn't have to worry about running into Phylicia all that much. With him outside measuring the strawboard that would replace the walls in the bedrooms, and her working inside in the front parlor, he hardly saw her for most of the morning. At noon, Jamal tossed the carpenter's pencil aside and entered the house through the door just off the kitchen.

He stopped at the arched entryway between the parlor and downstairs sitting room and watched as Phylicia carefully pried a section of aged wainscoting from the wall. She gingerly laid it next to an identical piece she'd placed on the floor, and turned to tackle the next section.

As she bent over, Jamal's hands fisted at the way the faded denim cupped her ass like a well-worn baseball glove. It probably felt as soft and smooth, too. He reined in the urge to walk up to her and test it for himself.

Stop it, he ordered himself. Phylicia had made her feelings known; he had to respect them, no matter how much it killed him to do so.

He shoved away from the doorjamb. "Are you hungry?" he asked.

She jumped and turned.

"Sorry," he said. "Didn't mean to sneak up on you."

"That's okay," she said. "Between the pounding and the music you'd have to wear a cowbell around your neck to announce your arrival." She smiled, and that urge to kiss her roared back to life. "Did you need something?" she asked.

And isn't that a loaded question?

Jamal bit back the answer that was on the tip of his tongue and held up his wrist to show her the time. "Lunch," he said. "What are you in the mood for?"

"Mine is in the truck," Phylicia answered. "I always bring my own lunch when I'm working on a site."

"Will you give me a few minutes to run over to Jessie's before you eat?" he asked, referring to the pseudo-restaurant that was run out of a local woman's kitchen. "I'm hoping you'll share some of the history of the house over lunch."

The look she gave him was guarded, as if she didn't trust his motives.

Smart woman.

He held his hands up. "Information. I promise I won't try anything else. I'll need to know the history of Belle Maison when giving tours to guests."

Slowly, she nodded, mistrust still evident in her narrowed gaze. "I'll wait for you. Let me know when you get back." She pointed at him. "But don't sneak up on me this time. It's not smart to startle a woman who's holding a crowbar."

"And I'm pretty sure you have several uses for it, too."

"Bet your ass I do." The musical sound of her laughter traveled along his skin like a caress. Jamal left the house before he went back on his promise not to try anything else with her.

"How long did you live here?" Jamal asked just as Phil took a bite of her sandwich. "Sorry," he said, obviously realizing what he'd done.

She held up a finger. While she chewed, she studied his legs that hung off the edge of the truck's tailgate, where they sat eating their lunch. The muscles were so well-defined they looked as if they were sculpted by hand. A faded four-inch line stretched across his knee.

"Surgery?" she asked, gesturing to it.

"Yeah, back in college. The bitter end to my dreams of playing in the major league."

"I forgot you played college baseball with Corey. That's how you two met, right?"

He nodded. "We were teammates for a couple of years. He was a junior when I was a freshman, but somehow we ended up being assigned together as roommates. Pissed him off, until the first care package from my mom arrived." He chuckled. "He warmed up to me after one bite of her famous walnut chocolate chip cookies."

"It must have been hard to see Corey go off to the majors," she said.

"He wanted it way more than I did," Jamal said with a casual shrug. "Playing major league baseball had always been my dad's dream. I just happened to be good at baseball, so I played it." He glanced at her. "I haven't admitted this to very many people, but when I went down with that knee injury I was more relieved than anything else."

"So, you spent most of your childhood trying to please your dad, too, huh?"

"You, too?" he asked.

"Oh, yeah. I was a total daddy's girl. He

hung the moon. Literally." Phil laughed. "Back when I was in grade school my room was decorated with a solar system motif," she explained.

"What was it like growing up here?"

"It was wonderful. Just look at it." She gestured toward the Victorian. "How many houses are so grand that they warrant a name? When I was younger, I used to pretend it was a castle."

"When did you move out?" he asked. "The Realtor said the house had been abandoned for some time."

"Unoccupied, not abandoned," Phil reminded him. "I lived at Belle Maison until I finished college. I went to Southeastern in Hammond, so I commuted back and forth. Who in their right mind would pick a dorm room over this, huh?"

"It sure beats that cubbyhole Corey and I shared back at Arizona State." He laughed. His head tipped to the side in inquiry. "What does a restoration specialist study in college? Did you get a degree in design?"

"No, finance." Phil rolled her eyes at his dumbfounded look. "I know, I know. How does a person with a finance degree end up restoring furniture?"

"It's not that big of a stretch. Corey told me the restoration business was your dad's.

Did you work in the finance world before joining the family business?"

"Nope." She shook her head. "I always knew this was what I wanted to do. But I figured I could help my dad grow the business with my finance degree."

But things had not worked out as she'd hoped. Phil could recall verbatim the argument she'd had with her dad over her vision for the company. If she had known it would be the last words she would ever say to him, she wouldn't have uttered half the things that came out of her mouth that day.

She took a sip of the iced tea Jamal had brought back from Jessie's. It had a hard time finding its way past the lump in her throat. "As I was saying, I lived here until I finished college. It was just me, Mom and Dad."

"This is a lot of house for three people," he commented.

"I know," Phil said, unable to suppress the nostalgic grin that drew across her lips. "According to the stories I've heard, my mom's grandfather had anticipated a large family, but after three wives and several mistresses, he only managed to produce one son. The largest brood was *my* grandfather's generation. There were four of them, but all of their descendants left Gauthier a long time ago. So the house passed down to my mom, and, eventually —" *unfortunately,* she thought "— to me."

Jamal assessed her for several long moments. "You hate that I'm the one who bought this house, don't you?"

"Yes," she answered, not even considering lying, but Phil was solicitous enough to soften the blow with a modest chuckle. "I don't mean to be harsh, but our styles differ a bit too much for my comfort. When I heard *you* were the new owner, I fully expected to find a wind turbine in the front yard."

Jamal's brow dipped with his chastising frown. "Everyone knows the wind turbine goes in the backyard next to the gazebo."

Phil nearly choked on her tea. She started to speak, but he stopped her with upraised palms.

"I'm kidding." He laughed. "There will be no wind turbine. I promise," he emphasized, humor still coloring his voice. "What do you have against saving the environment, anyway?"

"I don't have anything against saving the environment," she answered with an affronted frown. "I just don't like it when people ruin historic properties with their new-wave, save-the-trees green technology.

Belle Maison has been standing here for more than a century and a half. It's fine just the way it is."

"And I'll bet the utility bills are through the roof in the winter."

"Oh, for God's sake, this is south Louisiana, not Alaska. It may drop below freezing one week out of the year." Phylicia reined in her indignation, cautious of allowing her emotions to get the best of her.

Jamal held his hands up, as if he too recognized that things were getting too heated.

"Look," he started. "I get that you're big into restoration, but I'm just as passionate about my work. Can you at least *try* to embrace what I want to do? I promise you I will not disturb the integrity of the house."

"If you say so," Phil replied, unable to stanch the skepticism that dripped from the words, despite her best effort. "But I'll believe it when I see it."

Jamal rolled his eyes, chagrin blanketing his face. "You just wait," he said. "You'll hardly be able to tell the difference between my eco-friendly improvements and the original structure. That's what will be unique about my architectural firm, making the green technology unobtrusive."

"How long before you get your firm off

the ground?" she asked.

He shrugged again and stared at the house across the street for some time before answering. "Soon. I'm in no big hurry. My main priority is getting Belle Maison opened on time." He scooted off the back of the tailgate. "Which is why we should probably get back to work."

Something about the change in his tone gave her pause, but Phil didn't want to dig any deeper. The less she intruded into Jamal Johnson's life, the better.

She hopped down from the truck's tailgate. "Were you planning to strip the paint from the woodwork in the parlor?" she asked.

"I figured I didn't have a choice," Jamal answered.

"Let me see what I can do," she said. "I may be able to get it cleaned with the materials I have with me. If not, I can bring it back to my shop. Can you lay out some of that plastic sheeting over there?" She pointed to the area just off the gazebo.

He nodded and she went inside to grab a section of the wainscoting she'd removed. As Phil dabbed at the scuff marks with her least abrasive solvent, she surreptitiously studied Jamal as he sawed through panels of strawboard. Even though it was late

September, the temperature was still hovering in the upper eighties, and his sweat-soaked shirt clung deliciously to the muscles that undulated with every push of the saw.

It was mesmerizing, watching the sinuous motion of his shoulders rise and fall. Her hands itched with the need to glide along the moist, hot skin underneath.

He turned abruptly and caught her staring. Phil jumped, nearly knocking over the bottle of solvent.

"Careful there," he called, a knowing grin pulling at his lips.

"Oh, great," Phil muttered. Mortified, she lowered her eyes and got back to work.

A half hour later, Phil had managed to remove every scuff mark from the wainscoting without marring a single inch. Jamal walked over to where she stood and dropped to his haunches, observing her work.

"Unbelievable," he said with an awed breath. "How did you manage to get it clean without ruining the paint job?"

"I have my ways," she said.

He looked up at her, amusement sparkling in his eyes. "I can't wait to see what else you can do."

"Darling, I would blow your mind," she said before she could stop herself.

Way wrong thing to say. Phil inwardly

cringed, but she couldn't deny the shot of molten heat that flashed through her as Jamal's eyes took on a smoldering look. She knew she was skirting along the edges of the danger zone. After that kiss yesterday, the worst thing she could do was encourage his flirting.

Actually, that wasn't the worst thing she could do. The *absolute* worst thing would involve them both being naked.

Do not *think of him naked,* she mentally chastised.

Jamal rose slowly from his crouched position, his intense gaze searing straight through her. When he finally spoke, his voice was rough with want. "You can try to ignore this all you want, Phylicia. We both know it's there."

She didn't have to ask what *it* was. It was so apparent, so potent, it had nearly taken on a physical form. The attraction sizzling between them was hotter than her workshop after a full day of working with the blowtorch.

Phil swallowed past the lump in her throat. She wanted to shake her head. She was dying to tell him that she didn't want to ignore anything.

"That's too bad," she said, her voice so husky she barely recognized it. She cleared her throat. "Because I fully intend to ignore it."

Those sparks of electricity, like the kind zapping between them right now, were dangerous. She'd been burned before, and fear of making those same mistakes terrified her more than Phil thought possible.

This was all too eerily familiar to the severe lapse in judgment that had already caused her so much heartache. Standing here with Jamal, in the midst of a huge home-renovation project, was like a remake of a twisted reality show: *The Phylicia and Kevin Fiasco.*

How many times had Kevin crept up behind her while she was working and pressed his lips to her neck? It had taken little more than a gentle kiss and some sweetly whispered words before they were both stripping out of their clothes and making love among the dusty construction material.

She *so* was not going there again.

"Look, Jamal. I won't deny that there was some chemistry between us during Mya and Corey's wedding —"

"Not just at the wedding," he interjected.

"Okay, fine. The chemistry is still there. But I'm just not in the right place. Getting involved with you, with *anyone* right now . . . it's not going to happen. And don't even think about suggesting no-strings-attached sex," she added.

The broad grin that flashed across his face was pure sin. "I wasn't going to," he said. "But apparently you've been thinking about it."

Phil knew her face was as red as a fire engine. Why did he have to be so damn sexy?

"You're making a mistake," he said. "You and I both know that there's a lot more going on here than just the potential for no-strings-attached sex." He leaned forward and whispered in her ear. "Although that would be *a lot* of fun, Phylicia."

Lord, how she wanted to take him up on his offer!

It had been way too long since she'd had fun of any kind. And despite how doggedly she'd tried to suppress her body's outright craving for this man, all she had to do was look at him and she went liquid. More and more, the hazy figure that entered her nightly fantasies had started to solidify in her mind, and its strong jaw and deep brown eyes resembled one man. The one standing before her.

A slightly calloused thumb grazed her cheek then tipped her chin up. Phil stared at his sensually soft lips and bit back a needy moan.

"I don't want you to feel uncomfortable working here," Jamal said. "If your answer is no, then I'll just have to accept it. I'll survive. This isn't the first time I've been turned down by a pretty girl."

His noble capitulation only made her decision harder to swallow.

Phil was tempted to apologize for having to take such an uncompromising stance, but with everything else going on in her life, she could not summon the strength to deal with the complications that came with a relationship, even a casusal, no-strings-attached kind.

Because she didn't do casual sex. Her heart always managed to get involved. And eventually broken.

Stupid heart.

"Is this the last time we're going to have this conversation?" she asked.

"Yes," he answered. "I won't bring it up again. I don't think my tender ego can take another rejection."

He said it jokingly, but Phil was sure she saw genuine regret ghost across his face. For a minute she nearly relented, but that self-preservation instinct that had shielded her heart since Kevin's betrayal came to her rescue. Phil knew it was unfair to make

Jamal suffer for another man's wrongdo-
ings. She also knew she was cheating herself,
as well. But it was a price she was willing to
pay. She would not put herself through the
pain and humiliation she'd been through
with Kevin. A person could take only so
much.

CHAPTER 6

Phil pulled into the driveway of Mya and Corey's massive home in one of Gauthier's newer subdivisions. She parked behind a familiar black-and-chrome truck, and her heart rate immediately shot into the stratosphere. It had been three weeks since she'd started working with Jamal, and her infatuation with him had only intensified. Thoughts of the man invaded her mind on an embarrassingly frequent basis: while working at Belle Maison, as she browsed the aisles at LeBlanc's Supermarket.

In bed.

Oh, Lord. How she thought about him in bed.

If Jamal Johnson was half as good in real life as he was in her dreams, Phil doubted she could survive a night under the sheets with him. But that would never happen, so she was not entertaining the idea. Period.

"You are so weak," she mumbled.

Frustrated, Phil grabbed the spinach dip and chips she'd picked up from the grocery store and headed for the house. She could hear the raucous yells streaming in from the partially opened front door.

She stepped into the foyer, which quickly opened into a huge den. Every piece of furniture was occupied, with all eyes glued to the football game in progress on the wide flat-screen television mounted over the stone fireplace. Phil instantly spotted Jamal. He was the only person not garbed in the New Orleans Saints' colors of black and gold. Instead, he stuck out like a sore thumb in a red-and-white Arizona Cardinals jersey.

"You made it," Mya called from the loveseat.

Jamal looked back from his spot on the sofa and flashed a smile. Her blood started pumping faster.

Phil mentally groaned. She really had to work on controlling her body's reactions to him.

"I was just about to call you," Mya said as she approached.

"Sorry I'm late." Phil hugged her, barely getting her arms around her massively pregnant friend. "I had a couple of things to take care of before coming over."

"They're still in the first quarter," Mya

said, waving off her concern. She took the bag of chips from Phil and motioned for her to follow her to the kitchen. "Besides," Mya continued in a teasing voice, "I know how much you were just *dying* to come over and watch football."

"Been looking forward to it all week," Phil said with exaggeratingly false brightness.

A football fan she was not. But when Mya had asked her to join them for the always highly anticipated New Orleans Saints versus Atlanta Falcons game, Phil had agreed. It had been several weeks since she'd had a chance to hang out with her friend. After being apart for fifteen years, Phil was trying to make up for lost time with Mya.

"How are you feeling?" Phil asked her as Mya scooted onto a bar stool and snatched a pig-in-a-blanket from a tray.

"Fat," Mya answered. "And don't tell me I'm not."

Phil looked her up and down from across the bar. "I wasn't going to. We made a pact never to lie to each other, remember?"

Mya gasped. "Thanks a lot."

"Oh, stop it," Phil said. "You look gorgeous, and you'll have a cute little baby in just three months. That's worth whatever pounds you gain."

"I'm starting to think this baby doesn't like me," Mya said. "The way she kicks at night — I don't think they're your normal baby kicks. This little rascal has it in for me."

Phil slid off the stool and came around the bar. She rubbed Mya's burgeoning belly. "Don't call my goddaughter a rascal. She is going to be the perfect little lady, just like her auntie Phil. I already bought her a hammer with a pink rhinestone handle."

Mya laughed. "Speaking of hammers, how are things going with the restoration, Auntie Phil?"

"Okay." Phil shrugged.

"Just okay? Knowing Jamal, I'm expecting Belle Maison to look like something from *The Jetsons* cartoon. I'll bet you'll be able to turn the shower on from a keypad in the kitchen."

Phil rolled her eyes. "Please, don't give him any ideas. His strawboard walls and stockpile of squiggly fluorescent lightbulbs are bad enough."

"I knew the two of you would butt heads when it came to Belle Maison." Mya laughed. "To be honest, I'm still surprised you sold it. I always loved that house."

"So did I," Phil said.

Her conscience poked at her. She and

Mya didn't keep secrets from each other. Although Phil had learned that her friend had indeed kept a very big secret from her fifteen years ago — the fact that she'd gotten pregnant and miscarried Corey's baby back when they were in high school. But this was different. They weren't a couple of teenagers. But Phil wasn't sure she could handle it if Mya looked at her with derision when she learned how stupid Phil had been to land herself in such a bind.

Before she could say anything, Corey came into the kitchen, with Jamal following closely behind.

"You're missing a good game, baby," Corey said, planting a kiss on Mya's temple. He turned to Phil and gave her the same kiss. "What force of nature dragged *you* here to watch a football game?"

She nodded toward Mya. "The same one that used to drag me to the Gauthier High football games on Friday nights."

"You don't like football?" Jamal asked. He reached over and snagged a tortilla chip from the bowl on the bar, and his elbow brushed her arm. A shiver coursed through her body.

Okay, this was getting to be ridiculous. She'd worked side by side with the man for several weeks. Why in the hell were these

91

goose bumps traveling along her skin from a simple brush of his elbow? It was embarrassing.

Even so, Phil couldn't stop the rush of heat that came over her. She looked up to find a curious smile tipping up the corner of Mya's mouth.

Oh, great. That's just what she needed. She was tempted to claim a headache and go home, but knowing Mya, she would waddle her way over to Phil's house and hound her there.

Corey nudged Mya's arm. "Did you tell Jamal about the email you got yesterday?" he asked.

"Oh, right!" Mya said, twisting the bar stool to face Jamal. "I got an email from a church group in Alabama. They're considering stopping in Gauthier on their tour of the African American Heritage Trail at the end of November. Think we'll have somewhere for them to spend the night?"

Phil noticed the trace of apprehension that crossed Jamal's face.

"Yes," she answered before he had a chance to speak. He whipped his head around, his eyes wide with surprise. "The restoration is coming along pretty well, don't you think?" Phil asked him.

Jamal nodded. "Yeah, everything is running on schedule. It'll be open for business in time for the big tourist rush."

"I was tempted to head there today," Phil continued. "My time would have been better spent working over there than here watching football."

"What do you have against football?" Jamal asked.

Phil shrugged. "Same thing I have against catch-and-release fishing and playing marbles. I don't see a point to it."

"Phil's problem is that she doesn't understand the game. At all," Corey interjected. "I tried to explain football to her once in high school. That's an hour of my life I'll never get back."

"The rules make no sense," Phil argued. "How can you penalize someone for holding on to a player so that he can't tackle the guy with the football? Isn't that the players' jobs, to stop the opposing team from tackling the guy with the ball?"

"You *really* don't understand football." Jamal laughed.

"I've tried to learn it. It just doesn't make sense to me." She'd tried watching a game with Kevin once, but like Corey, he'd gotten frustrated and suggested she watch HGTV in the other room.

"I'll teach you if you really want to learn,"

Jamal said.

"Don't do it." Corey was shaking his head. "You don't want that headache."

Jamal shrugged off his friend's concern. "I'm serious," he said. "If you really want to learn, I'll go over some of the basics with you."

He looked so sincere, so genuine. Even though she had no interest whatsoever in learning more about football, Phil couldn't stop her heart from melting just a bit from his offer.

"Thank you," she said.

"Fumble!" someone shouted from the living room, and both Corey and Jamal took off running.

That coy grin still planted on her face, Mya emptied the store-bought spinach dip into a bowl. "Don't make me have to ask," she said.

"Ask what?" Phil tried for innocent.

Her best friend pointed a spoon at her. "Girl, you better start spilling. And I mean *right* now."

"There's nothing to spill," Phil said as she climbed back onto her bar stool. "I'm helping him with the house, nothing more. By the end of the day we are both tired and sweaty, and not in a good way."

"That is such a waste. Have you taken a

good look at that man?"

She slid her best friend an exasperated look. "I know how he looks, Mya. I've been staring at his ass for nearly a month."

"Well, stop staring and grab it," Mya said. "Come on, Phil. You're both single."

"We're both single? That's the best you can do?" Phil laughed. "My neighbor, Mr. Jenkins, is single. He's a grandfather and a widower, but still single. Should I ask him out?"

"You're both single and under the age of sixty-five," Mya said, heavy on the annoyance. "I'm being serious, Phil. Why wouldn't you give Jamal a chance? I'm sure the two of you have things in common."

"Like what?"

"Like architecture," Mya returned.

Phil nearly choked on a laugh. "Believe me, our take on architecture is definitely not something we have in common." She held her hands up when Mya started to speak again. "I know now that you're back with the love of your life you've developed this obsession with finding me a man, but it really isn't necessary, Mya. I'm perfectly content with my single status. Honestly, I have neither the time nor the energy for a relationship."

Mya frowned as she absently rubbed her

belly. "I just want you to be happy."

Phil gave her a cheesy fake smile. "I'm happy. I promise."

Mya leaned closer and whispered in a harsh breath, "The least you can do is sleep with him once so you can tell me how good he is."

"What makes you think he's any good at all?" she asked Mya.

They peered into the living room just as Corey and Jamal stood up and high-fived each other. His muscled arms and broad shoulders were displayed to perfection underneath the lightweight football jersey.

"Oh, yeah. He would be good," Phil said.

"So good," Mya agreed.

Phil was tempted. Good Lord, was she tempted. But she'd been burned once before. She needed to be smarter this time around. Her nightly fantasies would have to suffice.

Yet, even as the thought rolled through her head, another — this one just as strong — moved in.

Would it be a cardinal sin if she and Jamal saw each other outside of work?

Denying her attraction to him was harder than she'd ever imagined. She had not been this turned on by a man since . . . well . . . ever.

She'd convinced herself that she loved Kevin, but it had taken months of getting to know him before she'd felt even an ounce of the sizzle she felt when Jamal was near. It was primal, this awareness between them. Why not see where it would lead?

Because it will likely lead to heartache.

"Don't mix business with pleasure," she murmured.

"What was that?" Mya asked as she leaned back on the stool to watch the TV.

"Nothing," Phil answered. "Come on. I don't want you crashing to the floor."

They walked back into the den, and Jamal's eyes turned in her direction. He picked up his beer bottle and stared at her as he tipped it back, his eyes lit with a knowing, humorous glint.

Don't mix business with pleasure, Phil reminded herself. But the mantra became less and less convincing with every moment that passed.

Jamal balanced himself on the second rung from the top of the ladder as he stretched the tape measure to the bottom shingle.

"Are you trying to break your neck?" he heard from just below.

He twisted around so fast he had to latch on to the house to steady himself.

Phylicia ran to the ladder and held it in place. "Get down from there," she demanded.

"Just a minute." He quickly took the measurements he needed before making his way down the ladder. "Thanks for holding it steady for me."

"You do know better than to climb that high on a ladder without having a second person to anchor it, right? I know your comfort zone is usually behind a computer, but your family owns a construction company. You have to know at least that much."

"I know all the safety rules," he said. "I just needed a quick measurement."

Phylicia rolled her eyes. Jamal grinned. She was bossy as hell, but it looked so damn good on her.

"Was your client satisfied with the work you did on the radio?" he asked her.

She'd told him she would be a couple of hours late this morning because she had to deliver an antique radio she'd restored to a customer in Mandeville.

"My client was very satisfied," she said. "In fact, he hired me to restore an armoire that dates back at least a hundred years, I'm sure. It is an absolutely gorgeous piece. It's being delivered to my shop next week. But it won't interfere with my work here," she said. "I know we're under a huge time crunch."

"Since you came on board I've been able to catch up. I'm actually slightly ahead of schedule now. And once the work crew arrives in a few days, things will move even more quickly. Hey, what's with the frown?" Jamal asked.

"Nothing," Phylicia said. "Just sounds as if this job won't last as long as I thought it would."

"Yes, it will. That construction crew isn't touching the woodwork inside. That's a job for the much sought-after restoration specialist."

A modest grin curled the edges of her mouth. "Well, I guess the much sought-after restoration specialist had better get started then," she said, but she didn't move, just continued to stand there, her eyes locked with his.

Only a couple of feet separated them. Two steps. That's all it would take to bring their bodies into contact. Jamal took a step forward, and Phylicia immediately stepped back.

"I'll, um, get to work," she said before turning and disappearing into the house.

"Damn," Jamal said in a terse whisper. He had been so close. Why had he stalled? He should have just gone for it. What was the worst that could happen? She'd slap him? He'd take a slap in the face if it meant tasting those lips again.

He had to figure out a way to break through the roadblocks she continued to put up. He knew they would be good together, if only Phylicia would give them a chance.

But he wasn't ready to push the issue again. He was still raw from the last time she shot him down.

As usual, Jamal spent the morning working outside while Phylicia labored inside the house. Around noon, she came out, wiping her hands on a stained rag.

"Did you bring your lunch?" she asked.

"Yeah," he answered. "Didn't you?"

She shook her head. "I had to leave the house so early this morning that I forgot to pack something to eat," she said. "I was wondering if you maybe wanted to go over to Jessie's. It's fried okra day."

A ham sandwich, or sitting across the table from Phylicia eating some of the best food in Gauthier? Tough choice.

"I'll drive," Jamal said.

As they both climbed into his truck, Phylicia picked up the mail he'd tossed on the passenger seat. As he took the stack from her, she tapped the heavy, cream-colored one on top.

"Is that a wedding invitation?" she asked, gesturing to the envelope that had arrived from Arizona this morning.

"Yes," Jamal answered, a muscle automatically jumping in his cheek. "My sister's."

"Oh, that's wonderful. When is she getting married?"

"The Saturday before Thanksgiving," he said. He stuffed the invitation, along with the rest of the mail, into a compartment in the center console and backed his truck out of the driveway.

As he maneuvered around her dusty blue pickup, Phylicia said, "Hey, careful there. Just because it's a little banged up, don't think you can get away with swiping my fender. I know each and every scratch."

"I can tell you've had it for a while." Jamal laughed. "I'm guessing there's a reason you haven't upgraded?"

"It was my dad's," she stated the obvious. "That truck is as much a part of Phillips' Home Restoration as I am."

Jamal allowed several moments to pass before asking, "How did he die?"

Staring out the passenger side window, he barely heard her when she said, "Heart attack." She glanced at him with a somber frown, then brought her gaze back to the stalks of sugarcane lining the roadway. "He was fifty-nine," she continued. "Way too young."

Damn. That had to have been rough. "I'm sorry," Jamal said, wincing at the inadequacy of his words.

"Thanks," Phylicia said. "It hasn't been easy. Now that I think about it, his heart attack was the starting point of the three-year nightmare I've been living in."

Jamal glanced over at her. "Three years? What's caused your life to be a nightmare for the past three years?" he asked.

She dismissed his question with a wave. "Forget I even said that."

"No." Without thinking, Jamal reached over and covered her forearm. It felt as if he'd leaped over a huge hurdle when she didn't pull away. "You can talk to me," he said. "Why has life been a nightmare for you?"

"Jamal, I appreciate the concern, but I really don't want to get into any of that." She looked over at him. "Just let it go, okay?"

He nodded. He could respect her privacy. He had his own personal restricted area that he tried his hardest to avoid stepping into. Jamal could list at least a thousand things

he'd rather do than talk about his relationship with his father: roll around in a pile of
red ants, walk across cut glass with his bare
feet, leap out of a plane without a parachute.

Yet, he was willing to do all of those things
and more just to get Phylicia to share a bit
of her life with him. What was it about her
that intrigued him so damn much?

Maybe it was the fact that they were both
single and around the same age. It just
made sense that he would gravitate to her.

No, that wasn't it. Gauthier wasn't neces-
sarily a hub for potential dating prospects,
but he had his pick of available women.
Phylicia's draw was more than just a matter
of convenience. Something about her had
struck him from the very first moment they
had been introduced, and ever since the
evening they'd spent together after Corey
and Mya's wedding, he'd been downright
fascinated by her.

His cell phone trilled. Jamal slipped it
from his pocket, recognizing his Realtor's
number on the screen. He excused himself
and took the call, hanging up a minute later.

"Would you mind if we got our food to
go?" Jamal asked. "That was my Realtor.
She said she may have found the perfect
place for my architectural firm. I want to
check it out, make sure it's what I'm look-

ing for. We can pick up the food from Jessie's, and I can drop you back at Belle Maison."

"That's fine," she said. "Not like there's much else for me to do for the rest of the afternoon, anyway. I have to wait at least twenty-four hours for the stain on the molding to dry before it can be installed, and the part I need for the light fixture in the upstairs bathroom won't arrive until tomorrow."

"In that case, do you mind coming with me to see the house?" Jamal asked. "I could use the extra set of eyes, and you know exactly what to look for."

She sized him up, her shrewd eyes narrowing. "Is this al' part of some wicked plan to get me alone in the car with you for an extended amount of time?"

A smile broke out over Jamal's face. "You see straight through me."

"I don't want any funny business from you, Jamal Johnson."

"Are you sure about that?" he asked. "It would make the drive into the city so much more entertaining."

She gave him a pointed look.

Jamal released his grip on the steering wheel for a moment, holding his hands up in surrender. "Fine, no funny business.

Maybe."

Phylicia just shook her head and laughed.

A couple of weeks ago, she would have never agreed to take the hour-long drive into New Orleans with him. Jamal took it as a sign of progress. He was going to wear her down. Eventually.

As soon as he pulled up to the enormous house on Saint Charles Avenue, Jamal knew he was staring at the future home of J. Johnson Architectural Design. With its Renaissance-style balustrades, dome-shaped cupola and angled bay windows, the neo-classical Italianate structure encompassed everything there was to love about New Orleans's famed Garden District. This place felt . . . right.

The admission scared the hell out of him.

Nervousness, excitement, fear — they all swirled around his stomach, a gumbo of emotions that wouldn't let up. If this turned out to be the right spot, it would put him one step closer to realizing his dream.

Jamal swallowed past the uneasy lump that instantly formed in his throat.

"It's on the streetcar line. That's a huge plus right there," Phylicia said as she alighted from the passenger side. "And it's on the corner, so there's street parking both in the front and on the side."

"You're going to keep my pros versus cons list for me?" he asked.

"That sounds like a job for a personal assistant, and I am no one's assistant."

Jamal chuckled at her severe frown. "No, I can't see you taking orders from anyone."

"You'll need to hire an assistant soon, though," she said as they made their way up the walkway toward the mansion's covered portico.

Jamal gave a noncommittal grunt.

"You're not planning to be a one-man shop, are you? Not if you're thinking of housing your firm in something like this," she said, gesturing to the home that was no less than five thousand square feet.

"I'll eventually hire additional architects and a support staff, but it's still too early for me to think about that stuff."

She looked over at him, her head tilted slightly to the side. "You've been in Gauthier over a year already. When *will* you start thinking about it?"

The appearance of his Realtor saved Jamal from answering Phylicia's question. Which was a good thing since he wasn't sure if he even knew *how* to answer it. Opening this firm had been his dream for so long; the enormity of it caused his breath to hitch. It was a huge step. And, if he wasn't careful, it could be a huge *mis*step.

The Realtor gave them a tour of the stately home, with its polished hardwood floors and arched entryways.

"This is amazing," Phylicia said, running her fingers along a carved mantel. "Just look at the craftsmanship."

"This is characteristic of many of the homes in this neighborhood, isn't it?" Jamal asked.

She nodded. "The houses in this area were built around the same time period as Belle Maison." She looked over at him then dropped her face into her hands. "Oh, my God, you're going to ruin this place, aren't you?"

"Hey!" Jamal protested.

Her muffled voice held a painful edge. "Why? Why? Why?" she muttered. "Why don't you rent out some office space in the CBD?" Phylicia asked.

"I don't want to be in the Central Business District," he said, walking over to the fireplace. "And I will not ruin this house. I'm going to update it with more environmentally friendly materials."

Phylicia groaned, the sound not unlike a wounded animal being kicked in the stomach for good measure.

"The house is very sound, but could probably benefit from a bit of updating," the Realtor said.

"The whole point of my firm will be to combine the old with the new," Jamal explained. "I'll probably replace the windows with a more energy-efficient brand, and add insulation. I can cut the energy cost by more than thirty percent."

"If you can pull off something like that while maintaining the integrity of the house, you will have a lot of business coming your way," the Realtor said.

"Thank you," Jamal said. He turned to Phylicia. "At least someone thinks my ideas are good."

She just rolled her eyes.

As they continued their tour, Jamal pictured how he would set up the rooms. The first floor would house displays of green technology and a media room where he could show his clients video clips of how things worked. The second story would house the offices. The third floor was the perfect space for him to convert into living quarters for those days when he didn't want to make the hour-long drive back to Gauthier. The two bedrooms, bathroom, a small living area and decent kitchen would suit his needs just fine.

"So, what do you think?" the Realtor asked.

It was perfect.

In fact, the house was so perfect, he was tempted to drive to the bank and withdraw the money right now.

But something held him back, and it didn't take much soul searching to pinpoint just what it was.

Fear.

Jamal hated to put that label on it, but it could not be denied. It was the same fear that always traveled along his spine whenever he thought about finally getting serious about his firm. He hated that fear. And he knew exactly what was driving it, which made him hate it even more.

You can do this, he told himself. Despite his father's insistence that he wouldn't be able to succeed without falling back on the Johnson name, Jamal knew that he could make this architectural firm work.

But instead of the words *I'll take it* pouring from his mouth, Jamal said, "I'll have to think about it a bit more. Let me know if the owners get any more offers."

"Of course," the Realtor said.

He ushered Phylicia out of the house and climbed into his truck, then headed back toward the Pontchartrain Expressway.

"Would you mind taking a short detour?" Phylicia asked. "I want to see what they have at the Green Project in the Ninth Ward. They may have some pieces we can use at Belle Maison."

"The Green Project?" he asked.

"You mean you haven't heard of it? Mr. President of the Environmentally Friendly Club?"

"Uh-oh," Jamal said. "Will my membership be revoked?"

"It just might." Phylicia laughed. She guided him to the Saint Roch neighborhood, where the huge warehouse of reclaimed building material was located. They picked through vintage ironwork, brass doorknobs and bathroom fixtures, and even intricately wood-carved faceplates for light switches.

"I cannot believe you've never even heard of this place," Phylicia said. "I would have thought that as someone who's about to open an architectural firm specializing in green technology, you'd have scoped out places like this one."

"I'm sure I would have run across it eventually," he said. "I'm just not at that point in my plans yet."

"How far are you?" she asked.

Jamal looked up at her and shrugged. "I'm

still getting it all straight in my head."

"What's left to think about?" she asked. "You seem to be dragging your feet on this."

"Hey, what's with the third degree?" Jamal asked, his discomfort ratcheting up.

"I don't mean to pry —"

"Really?"

"— but what have you actually done to get your firm off the ground?" she continued. "You've got all these ideas for the business, but you're still just sitting on them. The thing that usually stops most people is the money, but you don't have that to worry about."

"It's not as if I'm in some huge rush," he said.

"Why aren't you?" she asked. "If this is what you really want to do. It *is* what you really want to do, isn't it?"

"Of course," Jamal said, unable to keep the defensiveness from coming through his voice.

"Are you sure this isn't like baseball? Is the architectural firm more your dad's dream than yours, Jamal?"

Jamal snorted a derisive laugh. "Oh, you are so off base it isn't even funny," he said.

Her forehead creased in annoyance, censure thinning those gorgeous lips.

Jamal released a weary sigh. He could tell

111

by the look on Phylicia's face that she had no intention of dropping the conversation.

"My father didn't agree with my decision to leave the family business," he told her. "He told me I was wasting my time trying to start a business from scratch when he'd already built an empire."

"Well, he has a point, doesn't he?" she asked, examining a set of copper-plated doorknobs. "Why build from the ground up when all the hard work has already been done? You can just incorporate your ideas for your firm into your family's company."

"That would never happen," Jamal said. "If you think you have a problem with this new-age green technology, just sit down and have a conversation with Lawrence Johnson."

"He can't be completely against it," Phylicia reasoned. "As much as I give you a hard time, I know there is merit to becoming eco-friendly. And, again, I am not completely against it. I agreed with your decision to add a solar water heating system, didn't I?"

He sent her a small grin.

"It was time for me to leave the family business," Jamal continued. "My dad and I were never going to see eye to eye, and he wasn't about to give up the reins to the company." He shrugged. "I didn't want to be under his thumb any longer."

"Which takes us back to my initial question. Why haven't you made more progress setting up *your* firm?"

Because if it failed, it would prove his father right.

He didn't say it — hell, this was the first time he'd allowed himself to mentally voice the thought — but, in his gut, Jamal knew that's what was holding him back.

He shrugged off her question, making him feel like a world-class coward. But he wasn't up for this discussion. Phylicia, on the other hand, just wouldn't let it drop.

"If you want to do it, I'd say it's time for you to go in one hundred percent. I'm not sure what you're looking for, but I think the house we just visited was phenomenal. On the pro versus con tally I've been keeping in my head, the pros far outnumber the cons," she said. "I think you should go for it."

"Will you be available to help me restore it?" he asked.

"There's nothing to restore," she said. "The house is in pristine condition."

"Hmm . . ." he said. "I guess I'll have to come up with another way to keep you around."

Her head reared back, her eyes blinking in surprise. "I didn't realize that was a priority on your list," she said.

"It is," Jamal assured her, holding her gaze for several long, heated moments.

She finally broke the connection, returning her attention to the crates of mismatched fixtures.

Jamal bit back a curse. For some reason, she didn't fully trust him. But they didn't know each other well enough for her to have formed a genuine opinion of him, negative or positive. Someone else had put that distrustful look in her eye — some bone-headed jackass who probably didn't deserve to be within the same airspace as Phylicia, let alone close enough to break her heart.

That also meant *he* would have to pay for the jackass's mistakes. As Jamal stared at her across a hodgepodge of brass knobs, he had no doubts that she would be well worth the effort.

They scored several articles to use in the restoration at Belle Maison. When they returned to the truck, Jamal popped the seat forward so he could store their finds in the truck's cab.

"Is that an instrument?" Phylicia asked, pointing to the case he kept behind the seat.

"A saxophone," Jamal answered.

Her eyes glittered with surprised humor. "I guess I shouldn't be shocked, although I wouldn't have pegged you for the woodwind section," she said. "Percussion, maybe."

"Is that a dig at my work with a hammer?"

"You do make more noise than the entire drum section of the Gauthier High School Marching Band."

Jamal shook his head. "You just love giving me a hard time, don't you?"

"It is a lot more fun than I ever imagined." She laughed as she slid onto the seat.

"So why doesn't it surprise you that I play the saxophone?" he asked as he backed out of the parking lot.

"Uh, let's see. Could it be because your entire iTunes collection seems to be filled with jazz?" she said.

"Not true. I've got some Tupac, a leftover from my rebellious days."

She barked out a laugh. "I'm not sure which one surprises me more, that you listened to Tupac or that you had a rebellious phase."

"I was the quintessential hell-raiser," he said. The look she slid his way told him that she didn't believe that for a minute. "Okay, so I *wanted* to be a hell-raiser. I just never got around to it."

That coaxed another musical peal of laughter from her. He would never get tired of hearing that sound.

"If you want to listen to something other than jazz, just let me know. You can give me your playlist and I'll download them."

"No, no," she said. "I love jazz."

"Really?" Jamal asked. "Now I'm the one who's surprised."

"Why's that? Were you expecting me to have Tupac's greatest hits?"

It was his turn to laugh. "No, I just didn't peg you as a jazz lover, either."

After a brief pause, she asked, "Have you been to any of the jazz clubs in New Orleans?"

Jamal shrugged. "A few months ago Wynton Marsalis had an exclusive performance at one of the clubs downtown. They only sold fifty tickets, so I was lucky to even get in. But I haven't checked out any others. I've been too busy, first with the renovations on my house, and now with Belle Maison."

"You live an hour away from the birthplace of jazz and have only been to one club?" She tsked. "That is unacceptable, Mr. Johnson."

"I know," he said with a healthy amount of shame in his voice, causing her to chuckle.

After another pause, she said, "Maybe we should go sometime."

Jamal did a double take. "Did you just ask me out? Like on a date?"

"Don't make a big deal out of it," she said.

"The hell I won't. You just asked me out on a date!"

"Yes, I asked you out on a date," Phylicia said with a sigh. She stared at him for several long moments, and in a voice that held more uncertainty than he'd ever heard from her, she asked, "Should I take it back?"

"Hell no," he said.

Her lips curled at the edges, and Jamal's mind instantly conjured that kiss he'd stolen in her workshop. He recalled the taste as if it had just happened.

"Good," Phylicia said. Then she turned her eyes back to the road ahead.

Jamal knew he should pay more attention to the road, too, since he was the one driving, but his eyes continued to stray to her profile. Gorgeous didn't do her justice. With those high cheekbones and elegant neck, she was *so* past gorgeous. She was stunning. Striking. Sexy.

And she'd just asked him out.

"So, what kind of date will this be?" he asked. "Are you doing this just because you want me to experience more jazz music, or is this a *date* date, as in we sit and share a meal that doesn't come on a disposable plate?"

After a slight pause, she said, "I was hoping it could be a *date* date."

Jamal lost a bit of the air from his lungs.

"I know I'm the one who asked for the hands-off rule," Phylicia continued. "But when we were at Mya's for the game on Sunday, she said something that got me thinking. We are both two single adults, in a town that doesn't have many single adults our age. What's wrong with the two of us going out for a night on the town?"

"Not a damn thing," Jamal said with a smile he couldn't hold back if he tried. "So, when will this date happen?" he asked.

"When are you available?"

"Right now," Jamal answered without hesitation.

Her head flew back, her sharp laugh reverberating around the truck cab. "I doubt there are any clubs open right now."

"Tonight then?"

"You want to go to a jazz club on a Wednesday night? Wouldn't Friday or Saturday be the more traditional date nights?"

"To hell with tradition," Jamal said. "Don't make me wait until the weekend, Phylicia."

She twisted a bit in her seat, turning

toward him. "Okay," she said. "I guess it isn't unheard of to go out in the middle of the week. The clubs should be less crowded."

"So will the restaurants."

"We really don't have to go out to dinner," she said.

"If I'm taking you out on a *date* date, I'm buying you dinner. That's non-negotiable."

She rolled her eyes. "Will you insist on opening the car door for me and pulling out my chair, too?"

"I can do that," he said. "I had the finer points of being a gentleman drilled into me at a very early age." He slid a sly smile her way. "It wasn't until high school that I learned when it's okay not to be a gentleman."

A decidedly wicked smile drew across her lips. "Hmm . . . maybe I'll get to see both sides to you tonight."

His stomach pulled tight, and the breath that was on its way out of his lungs stalled. Jamal was pretty sure he wouldn't notice if a nuclear bomb erupted right in front of him, and if it wasn't for fear of running them off the road, his tongue would be in her mouth right now.

Hopefully, he would get the chance to experience that tonight.

He pulled into the driveway of Belle Maison and Phylicia hopped out. She walked around to the bed of the truck, but Jamal stopped her before she could grab any of the items they'd picked up from the salvage yard.

"I've got this," he said. "Why don't you go home and get ready?"

"Is this your polite way of saying that I'll need extra time to get prettied up before you take me anywhere?"

"You don't have to do a damn thing to yourself, Phylicia. It's impossible for you to get any more beautiful."

Her smile turned even more wicked. And playful. And kissable.

She tilted her head to the side, her eyes sparkling with mischief. "If you're trying to flatter your way into my pants, it just might work." She started for her truck, calling over her shoulder, "I'll see you tonight."

CHAPTER 7

Phil turned onto the winding road that led to Mossy Oaks Care Facility, traveling under the canopy of moss-laden oak trees that shaded the drive. She rounded a curve, and the yellow-and-white French Chateau-style building came into view. It looked more like a resort hotel than a 24/7 care facility for dementia and Alzheimer's patients.

Phil signed in at the front desk, taking a couple of minutes to chat with Evelyn, the receptionist who made her mother homemade praline candies at least once a month. Phil was completely indebted to this staff. Just thinking about the care they bestowed upon her mother made her throat tighten with gratitude.

When she reached her mother's room, Phil found her staring out the window at the grounds below.

"Mom?" Phil called.

Her mother turned. Sabina Phillips looked at least five years younger than her sixty-two years. She smiled, and hope blossomed within Phil's chest.

"Hello, Agatha," her mother returned.

Phil managed to suppress the defeated sigh that nearly escaped. She'd prayed for a rare glimpse of lucidity today.

"No, Mom, it's me, Phylicia," she said, walking over to her. She took her mother's hands and led her to the small seating area, gesturing for her to take the seat that provided the same view of the grounds.

Phil often wondered what her mother saw when she looked out there. Did she recognize the people as the same residents she dined with on a daily basis, or were they strangers to her addled brain, as her own daughter had become?

Phil pulled in a deep breath and pasted on a smile.

"How are things going today?" she asked.

"Oh, I'm good. I loved the strawberry preserves you made for me, Agatha. I can never get Mama's recipe right."

Phil contemplated pushing her mother to remember, but decided against it. She didn't have much time for this visit, and if she pushed too hard, her mother would likely become agitated. She would be her aunt Agatha today, even though her mother's younger sister had died of breast cancer over a decade ago, at the young age of forty-eight.

"Did you eat the preserves the way you usually like them?" Phil asked.

Her mother's smile took on a mischievous edge as she nodded. "Over ice cream. I spent the entire week picking up after Percy. I figure I deserved a treat."

"Nothing wrong with treating yourself," Phil said. "And Percy appreciates you picking up after him."

"Oh, I know he does." The smile turned naughty. "He has his ways of showing me."

Okay. They so were not going there. In these past few years, ever since her mother had begun to mistake her for her aunt Agatha, Phil had learned way more about her parents' very healthy sex life than she *ever* wanted to know, especially since she wasn't carrying on in the family tradition.

"You need to get rid of that no-good man of yours," her mother said. "If Lewis doesn't want to marry you after fifteen years, he never will, Agatha."

"I know," Phil answered. Her aunt's longtime on-again/off-again boyfriend had made Kevin look like a prime catch. One thing she could say about Kevin was that he had never cheated on her, as far as she knew, anyway.

Phil hesitated a moment before saying, "I have gotten rid of him." She bit her lower lip. "I'm, uh, seeing someone else."

Her mother's eyes widened. "Really? Who is he? Someone I know?"

"He's pretty new to town," Phil answered. "But he's very sweet. And I really like him. A lot."

"Oh, Agatha. I'm so happy for you. Does he treat you well?"

"So far," Phil said. "We're going on our first date tonight."

Sabina sprung from the chair. "So what are you doing here? You should be getting ready for your date." She captured Phil's wrist and pulled her up from the chair. "You can come back later and tell me all about it. We'll have time to chat. Percy will be in his workshop all day, doing his best to turn my baby girl into a tomboy."

"Hey, she's not *that* much of a tomboy," Phil interjected.

"She's just like her daddy. But Phylicia loves it, so I don't mind."

Phil's heart became so full it hurt. "You were always so understanding," she said, running a finger gently down her mother's cheek. She pulled in a deep breath. "I'll be

124

back in a few days. We'll have some of that ice cream."

"Okay, Aggie," Sabina said. "You have a good time tonight."

Phil kissed her mother's soft cheek. "I love you, Mom," she whispered.

Despite ordering herself not to cry, her cheeks were soaked by the time she backed her truck out of the parking space.

"Why even bother with a bra?"

Phil twisted around, her hand still in her underwear drawer. "What's that supposed to mean? Just because I don't have giant pregnant-woman breasts doesn't mean my girls can just go free."

Pulling a tissue from the box she'd brought with her, Mya blew her nose with one hand and pointed at Phil with the other. "Jamal would appreciate your girls a lot more if they were not bound."

"Are you taking something for that cold?" Phil asked, ignoring her friend's base, although probably true, statement.

"Can't." Mya pointed to the beach ball she seemed to be hiding underneath her stylish running suit. She adjusted the pillows stacked up against the headboard, then grabbed the potato chip bag and stuffed a chip in her mouth. "Do you know where he's taking you to eat?" Mya asked.

"I'm not sure." Phil exchanged the light gray slacks she'd taken out for a pair of dark blue jeans. "I told him I was in the mood for seafood."

"Oh, that sounds good," Mya moaned. "Maybe he'll take you to Commander's Palace, or Galatoire's."

"No way," Phil said.

"You wanna bet?" Mya asked. "Jamal doesn't do things halfway. He's loaded. And when I say loaded, I mean *loaded.*"

"I don't care," Phil said. "First of all, it's a *first* date. It would be just plain rude to accept some fancy dinner. And, secondly, he's currently my employer."

"Not tonight," Mya said.

"And thirdly," Phil talked over her, "I don't want him thinking that he can get payment in another form in return for an expensive meal."

"Must I remind you that getting a little action down there would not be a bad thing for you? Unfortunately, Jamal isn't the kind of guy who'd take advantage of you. He's one of the good ones."

Phil looked up and caught Mya's eyes in the mirror. "I think so, too," she said. She let out an exasperated breath and plopped down on the bed. "I really like him, Mya."

"Aw, honey, that's a good thing," Mya said, rubbing Phil's back. "Why do you look as if you lost your favorite toy?"

Phil drew comfort from the concern she heard in her best friend's voice. How many times had this scenario played out between them when they were teenagers? Mya trying to ease Phil's worries over some boy.

"I just don't want to get hurt," Phil finally admitted.

"Oh, sweetheart." Mya tossed the bag of chips onto the bed and scooted over to her side. She wrapped her arms around Phil's shoulders and gave her a sisterly squeeze. "If I ever meet that Kevin person I will kick his ass."

Phil snorted a laugh. "You'd have to get in line."

"Forget about him." Mya brushed a wayward curl from her brow. "Tonight is about starting over, and Jamal is an excellent person to start with."

"God, I hope you're right." Phil sighed.

"He is. Just give him a chance."

Giving Mya another hug, Phil got up from the bed and stepped into her jeans. She pulled on a silky halter top with a ribbon of sequins that sat just below her breasts. It wasn't her usual style, and completely wrong for October, but it was unseasonably warm this year and would probably be even warmer in the jazz club.

She slipped into a pair of superhigh heels — an impulse buy — and turned when Mya let out a high-pitched whistle.

"I cannot wait to see Jamal's face when he picks you up."

"What's the big deal?" Phil asked.

"You! Look at you! You look like you belong on a damn runway. Tight jeans, a sexy top and the fiercest *do me* heels I've ever seen." Mya pointed an accusing finger at her. "Don't think I don't know what you're doing, Phylicia Phillips. You are trying to drive that man out of his mind."

"No, I am not," Phil protested, turning to the cheval mirror that had been in her family for generations. She looked over her shoulder at Mya and admitted, "Well, maybe a little."

"I know you!" Mya laughed so hard she started to cough.

Phil ran over to her and patted her back. "Take it easy, will you? Corey's not going to murder me for letting his pregnant wife die on my watch."

She returned to the mirror to touch up her hair and makeup. A few minutes later, the doorbell chimed, and her stomach did a double somersault.

"Ooh, I'll get it," Mya said, mimicking a crab as she gave a valiant effort to climb off the bed.

Phil stopped her. "He'll think no one's home if he has to wait for you to get to the door." She was embarrassed at the way she nearly raced to the front door, then colossally disappointed when she opened it to find Corey standing on the other side.

"Wow." His eyes ballooned as he looked her up and down. "Who knew *that* was hiding under those coveralls?"

Phil gave him a playful slap on the arm. Whether it was payback for his gibe, or because he wasn't Jamal, she hadn't decided yet. The jitters tingling along her skin in anticipation of his arrival were completely ridiculous. She'd just seen the man a few hours ago.

"Where's my wife?" Corey asked. "She eat all your food yet?"

"I've still got a few grapes and some yogurt left," Phil answered, gesturing for Corey to follow her to the bedroom.

"Hey, you," Mya greeted him, patting the bed next to her.

Corey stopped just outside the door and shook his head. "I'm not coming in there. Too much estrogen."

"Coward," Mya and Phil said at the same time.

The doorbell rang again, and Phil literally jumped. So did her heart. Then it started racing triple-time.

"Oh, oh, oh! Phil's date is here!" Mya said, clapping her hands like a five-year-old.

"Which means we should probably go out the back door," Corey said.

Thank you, Phil mouthed over Mya's head as her friend waddled out of the bedroom, complaining about not being there for the big reveal.

Phil took a moment to collect herself before making her way to the foyer. She waited until she'd heard the back kitchen door close behind Corey and Mya before opening the front door. Those darn tingles instantly sprung along her skin at the sight of Jamal. He wore a lightweight sweater and tan slacks, and he looked good enough to eat.

His eyes widened. "Damn," he blew out on a heavy breath.

"Was that a good damn or a bad one?" Phil asked.

"Definitely a good one," he said. "You look amazing, Phylicia."

"I think it's because you're used to seeing me with sawdust in my hair." She fingered one of the loose curls that framed her face, and in a teasing voice said, "I washed it for you. You should feel really special."

"I do," he said with a sexy smile.

She smiled back. She couldn't help it. After a moment that lasted way too long, yet not nearly long enough, Phil shook her head. "I'm sorry. Come on in while I grab my purse."

He followed her, his hands in his pockets. His eyes roamed around the open living room/dining room/kitchen area. "Nice house," he said. "Though, to be honest, I can't picture you living here."

"Why's that?" Phil asked over her shoulder.

"You restore historic homes for a living. I'm surprised you can be comfortable in something this modern."

Phil shrugged. "I doubt I'll live here forever, but for now, it's home."

Jamal stopped short. "You were planning to move back into the Victorian, weren't you?"

Yes, she had been planning to eventually return to Belle Maison, but one look at the distress on his face and Phil decided to spare him.

"You were," he said in a pained voice.

"Don't worry about it," she said. "The

131

house is yours, Jamal. You paid a nice sum of money for it. Believe me, I know what the asking price was." Phil gestured for him to follow her. "Come on. I haven't eaten since lunch. I'm starving."

He stood there for a few more moments, that mixture of regret and apology in his eyes. If he said one more thing about the house, she would scream. But he didn't. Instead, he walked over to the door and held it open for her.

"After you."

Jamal sat at the Formica-topped table at Mother's Restaurant, watching Phylicia as she bit into her sandwich. How he could be so turned on by a woman with gravy running down her chin, he didn't know.

Actually, he did. Sitting across from him, she looked downright edible.

"This isn't exactly what I had in mind for dinner," he commented, looking around the understated dining room that was just a step up from Jessie's carport. "But this food proves that you should never judge a book by its cover."

"I cannot believe you've lived here over a year and have never eaten a po'-boy from Mother's," Phylicia said. "Presidents have eaten here. It's legendary."

"As evident by that never-ending line." Jamal pointed to the stream of people still filtering in. They'd waited in that line for more than an hour, but it hadn't been a hardship with Phylicia as company.

"You were telling me about how you and Mya managed to get yourselves arrested," he said. "We're not leaving until I get the rest of the story."

She rolled her eyes. "We didn't get arrested. At least charges were never filed. Mya's grandpa smoothed things over with Mrs. Jackson by promising to bring her fresh vegetables from his garden for a year."

"But you stole the woman's car."

"We *borrowed* her car," Phylicia said. A sneaky smile drifted across her face. "I still can't believe we did that. It was all Mya's fault. No, actually, it was Corey's fault. He's the one who went to baseball camp in Covington for an entire month and told Mya he would explode if he didn't see her. And, like the love-struck fool she was, she went running."

"And you helped her. What does that say about you?"

"Who was I to crush young love?" she said with a laugh. "Anyway, we never told Mya's grandpa exactly why we took Mrs. Jackson's car. He probably would have had Corey locked up if he knew."

"Is that the most trouble you've ever gotten into?" he asked.

She nodded as she forked a helping of potato salad. "I was a pretty good kid. There wasn't too much mischief to get into in Gauthier. What about you?" she asked. "Were you a troublemaker?"

Jamal shook his head. "I was the apple of my parents' eyes." Too bad that apple had started to rot over the past few years, at least as far as his father was concerned. "I had ample opportunity to get into trouble, but it just never interested me," he said. "I was too busy trying to learn as much as I could about that eco-friendly stuff you hate so much."

"I told you before that I don't hate it. I just think it has its place."

"Which happens to *not* be in the Victorian, right?" He laughed. "You're going to be impressed with the way I integrate this new technology into that house."

"It takes a lot to impress me," she returned, taking a sip of her iced tea.

"I guess I have my work cut out for me," he murmured.

The air crackled with electric heat. It pulsed like a living, breathing entity between them.

"Are you ready to head to the club?" Phylicia asked.

They had walked to the restaurant from the prime parking spot Jamal had found just a few yards away from the jazz club in the French Quarter. Mirroring the route they'd taken, they turned left down South Peters Street, walking past the bright lights of Harrah's Casino. They made their way along Decatur Street, maneuvering around a crowd that had gathered to watch a couple of street performers. Jamal took a chance at reaching for her hand and experienced an overwhelming sense of accomplishment when she didn't pull away but instead threaded her fingers with his.

"You ever work on any of these buildings?" he asked as they strolled along Saint Ann Street in the heart of New Orleans's most famous neighborhood.

"Several of them." She nodded. "My dad and I used to drive into the city at least twice a month to do restoration work."

"You enjoyed working with him." It was more a statement than a question.

"Absolutely," she said. "I never considered doing anything else. It's been a part of me for as long as I can remember."

"I can tell how much you love it. It shows in the care you take when you work," he elaborated.

"Thank you," Phylicia replied. "It means a lot to hear that. My dad left some pretty big shoes to fill, and I'm working as hard as I can to fill them."

"You think he would be proud of what you've done with the business?"

Her mood changed almost instantly, a shuttered look coming over her face.

"What's wrong?" he asked. Because something was definitely wrong.

She looked over at him and shook her head. "You just hit the sensitive button," she said, but her somber smile told Jamal a whole lot more than her words.

Just when he thought she would try to change the subject, Phylicia squeezed his hand and said, "My dad and I were closer than any two people I know. I suspected that he'd wished I was a boy, but he never let me feel unwanted. In fact, he spoiled me rotten. I could get away with just about anything.

"From the minute I could grip a putty knife, I was in the workshop with him, handing him tools."

"So, what happened?" Jamal asked, running his thumb along her smooth skin.

"We had different ideas about how to handle the business," she said. "I thought it was time Dad branched out, hired additional people so we could take on bigger jobs. He didn't agree." She pulled in a deep breath. "My last conversation with him was a huge fight over the direction we should take the business. He died a couple of hours after I stormed out of his workshop. I would do anything to have that day back," she finished in a small voice.

"Your heart was in the right place," Jamal said.

"I know," she said. "So did Dad. It still doesn't erase what happened."

He wanted to pull her into his arms and hold her. He'd never seen Phylicia so vulnerable, and bastard that he was, he wanted to take full advantage of it. Having her emotions so exposed, it was hard not to give in to the need to comfort her.

"I'm sorry," she said with a delicate sniff. "Talk about a way to ruin a first date."

"You haven't ruined anything," he said. "I know a thing or two about having regrets, especially where family is concerned."

She looked up at him and squeezed his hand. In that moment, Jamal had never felt a deeper connection to a woman. It transcended mere attraction, burgeoning into something more profound.

"We're here," Phylicia said as they came

upon a nondescript building with a simple green door. "Are you ready to hear some of the best undiscovered jazz musicians in the city?"

If it meant spending more time with her, he'd listen to a band of out-of-tune bagpipers.

Jamal opened the door, settling his hand at the small of her back as he urged her to go ahead of him. As the heat of her skin penetrated her silky top, Jamal tried to think of anything that could be better than being with her tonight.

He couldn't come up with a single thing. Tonight had been everything he'd hoped it would be . . . and they were only halfway through it.

CHAPTER 8

The sultry sounds coming from the jazz quartet filtered through the cozy bar, creating an intimacy that was hard to ignore. As they danced, Phil concentrated on the muscles beneath her fingers as she held on to Jamal's solid back.

She couldn't remember the last time a man had looked at her with the same intensity as Jamal was looking at her right now. He ran one hand down her spine, stopping just above her waist. She was tempted to take his hand and move it lower until his warm palm cradled her backside.

Instead, she put her arms around Jamal's neck and rested her head on his shoulder.

"You feel amazing," Phil said on a sigh.

His body went rigid. When she peered up at him, his eyes were heavy with heat. "I can't put into words how it feels to have you against me, Phylicia. I've been dreaming about this ever since Mya and Corey's wedding."

So had she. He had taken top billing in her nightly fantasies even before the wedding. It had only intensified after the hours they'd spent together that night.

In a hushed whisper, he asked, "What did I do wrong?"

"What do you mean?"

"We had such a good time that night, and then nothing. Why did I become enemy number one?"

Contriteness heated her face. "I owe you an apology for the way I treated you," she said. "It was unfair."

"Why did you?" he asked.

She looked down at his chest, then back at his eyes. "It was because of the house," she finally answered. "I found out the day after the wedding that you were the person who'd bought it. If I'd seen you that day, I probably would have run you down with my truck. That's just how livid I was."

"I had no idea you were trying to buy the house," he reiterated.

"I know you didn't," she said. "I had no right to blame you, but I did anyway."

"Phylicia, how did you end up losing the house?" he asked.

She shook her head. "Don't. Not right now. Tonight has been too perfect. I don't want to mess it up."

"But —"

She placed her fingers on his lips, silencing him. They felt warm against her skin, almost as warm as his eyes, which were so heated they nearly singed her. The raw desire so evident in his penetrating stare set her blood ablaze.

She wanted this man. She'd wanted him from the moment she'd met him. And it was more than obvious that he wanted her, too.

"You're not very good at hiding what you're thinking," Phil murmured.

"I'm not trying to hide it," he returned, his voice rough with lust.

She moved closer to him and rested her head against his broad chest. As they swayed back and forth to the bluesy sound of the trumpeter's song, she couldn't help but imagine doing this a thousand times more. She felt at home in his embrace, as if he was a missing puzzle piece that she hadn't realized fit until she'd stepped into it.

"Thank you for tonight," she murmured against his chest. She tilted her head up slightly, just long enough to send him a grateful glance. "It's been so long since I've been out dancing. I really needed this."

"You're welcome," he said. "We can do it again, and again, and again. Until you're good and satisfied."

They were no longer talking about dancing. Goose bumps broke out across Phil's skin. Her nipples pebbled, pulling tighter with each brush against Jamal's solid chest.

The trumpeter's ballad waned with a final, haunting note. When she pulled away to applaud the musicians, her body mourned the loss of feeling Jamal against her. They returned to their table, which had remained unoccupied with the small Wednesday night crowd.

"Wow, it's almost midnight," she commented. Phil had resisted checking the time, not wanting the night to come to an end.

"It's a good thing midnight is considered still early in this town," he said.

"Even when I have to get up at six in the morning?" She sent him a sly grin. "My boss might get upset if I show up late or fall asleep on the job tomorrow."

Jamal chuckled. "I think he'll cut you some slack."

"Probably because he's planning to sleep in himself?" she asked.

"If I can sleep at all. I think I'll be reliving tonight in my head for many nights to come."

And wasn't *that* just the thing to say to send shivers down her spine?

"You may have a degree in architecture, but I think you minored in being a sweet-talker," Phil joked.

"Actually, I minored in music," he returned.

Her brow lifted. "So it's not just a hobby."

He shook his head.

"Are you as good as that guy?" she asked, nodding toward the saxophonist on stage.

Jamal looked over his shoulder. "Only one way for you to find out," he said. He pushed up from the chair. "I'll be right back."

"Wha—" Phil stared at his back as he exited the club. Several minutes later, he returned, saxophone case in hand. "Oh, my goodness," she said.

Jamal bypassed their table and headed for the stage. He spoke with the man who sat on a stool at the base of the stage, nodded, then looked back at her, flashing a smile as he climbed the steps and stepped up to the lone microphone.

"I don't mean to usurp anyone's time here on stage," he said into the microphone, "but this happens to be a pretty special night. I hope the crowd doesn't mind if I serenade my date with a special song, just for her."

"Oh, my goodness," Phil whispered again. She glanced around her, self-conscious as several of the people in the club sent smiles her way.

She should kick his butt for this. But honestly, who had ever done something so sweet?

When the first notes drifted from Jamal's sax, Phil forgot about the people surrounding them. He played with passion, the perfect notes weaving their way around her.

His eyes were closed as he leaned over his instrument and stroked his fingers along the brass keys. Every so often he'd look up at her, a smile lighting his eyes. Tremors of awareness traveled along her spine, as if the pads of his fingers were moving up and down her skin instead of the saxophone.

When Jamal drew out the last note, applause drifted around the half-filled club. He accepted the praise with a nod and thanked the musicians for allowing him to encroach on their space.

Phil stood and gently applauded him when he returned to the table.

"So?" he asked when he resumed his seat at the table. "Was I any good?"

"I can't even joke about it. You were better than I ever imagined."

"Thank you," he said.

"Really, I wasn't expecting that. You don't just dabble in music. You're good enough to be featured here or at any of the other jazz clubs around the city."

"I wouldn't say that," Jamal said with true modesty, "but I do love it. I always have. Music has always been my escape."

She tilted her head to the side and studied him for several beats. "What have you had to escape from?" she asked.

"Not tonight," he said, using the words she'd used earlier. "Let's save that conversation for another time."

"Fair enough," Phil said. She felt the same way. The night had been too magical to mar it with unpleasant thoughts. But, unfortunately, it was time to bring their magical night to an end.

"It really is time to head back," she said in a mournful tone. "We have an hour's drive ahead of us."

"We can stay in the city," he said. Phil's eyes widened at the suggestion.

"In separate rooms," he added, then tacked on, "if that's what you want."

What she wanted and what she would agree to were two totally different things. She wanted to take him by the hand and lead him to the nearest hotel room, but she'd allowed her body to rule once before, and she was still paying for it.

"I think we should head back to Gauthier. We both have a long day ahead of us."

His disappointment was blatantly obvious, but to his credit, Jamal didn't push, nor did he sulk, which was what Kevin would have done. Ever the gentleman, he paid their tab and, with his hand on the small of her back, guided her out of the club.

"Thank you," Phil said as he held the door to his truck open for her.

"Thank *you,*" he returned, wedging his body inside the truck cab and buckling her into the seat. "It's been a while since I played my saxophone for anyone but myself. Thanks for giving me the opportunity."

He leaned forward and pressed a swift, hot kiss against her lips, then closed the door. Phil's eyes tracked him as he rounded the front, opened the door and climbed into the truck.

"It was okay that I did that, right?" he asked.

"The kiss?"

He nodded.

After a pause, she said, "It's okay."

He looked over at her. "Is it okay if I do it again?"

A smile curved up the sides of Phil's mouth. She unbuckled the seat belt and scooted over to his side. Then she wrapped her hand around Jamal's neck and tilted his head toward her.

"Just remember, if I'm too tired to work tomorrow, you'll have to answer to my boss."

"I think he'll understand," he said as he dipped his head and captured her lips in a much slower, much deeper kiss.

A soft sigh escaped her throat as Jamal's tongue eased into her mouth, exploring with a relaxed familiarity that shouldn't have been possible after so few kisses, yet seemed . . . right. As if his mouth belonged there, connected to hers.

Phil snaked her free hand up his chest, fanning her fingers out against his solid, warm muscles. She pressed herself more firmly against him and rubbed her knee against the prominent bulge in his lap.

Jamal tore his mouth from hers and let out a loud groan.

"Okay, maybe we should stop before we get in trouble," he said.

She really wasn't in the mood to stop, but Phil knew he was right. Anyone could pass the car and see them going at it like a couple of teenagers. Her days of making out in cars were behind her. She was a grown woman with her own house. They could make out there.

Actually, they could do a lot more than make out.

147

"You're right," she said. "I think you should take me home."

His one-handed grip on the steering wheel tightened to the point that Jamal figured he'd leave indentions in the hard plastic. They were nearing Phylicia's place, and if it were an option, he'd give up his house, his car and most of the money in his bank account for the chance to follow her inside.

He pulled into her cul-de-sac and, moments later, turned into her driveway.

They spoke over each other.

"Can I —"

"Do you —"

She gestured for him to go first.

"I was just going to ask if I could walk you to your door," Jamal said.

"I was going to ask if you wanted to come in for a few minutes. I know it's late —"

"Absolutely," Jamal answered. Did she really think she had to convince him to follow her into that house?

He got out of the truck and raced around the front to open her door, but as she'd done earlier, she'd already gotten out. His chivalry was useless on her. She pulled the key out of her small clutch purse, and Jamal followed her inside.

Still silent, they made their way to her

kitchen. "Have a seat," she said, pointing to one of the stools at the angled bar that separated the living room from the kitchen. "Can I get you a drink? Beer? Wine?"

Jamal declined the offer. "The two beers are my limit when I'm driving. Actually, they're pretty much my limit, period. I'm not much of a drinker. I'll take a bottle of water," he said.

"You're so responsible," she said, grabbing a couple of bottled waters from the refrigerator.

"Is that a good thing or a bad thing?" Jamal asked.

"It's good. I'm not a fan of men who back out on their responsibilities."

Don't bring it up. Do not bring it up.

"Are you speaking from experience?" he asked, and immediately felt like an idiot. Why in the hell did he bring it up?

She sipped from her water bottle, staring at him as she tilted her head back slightly. She capped the bottle and set it on the counter next to her. "Maybe," she answered. "That's another topic I'd rather not get into tonight."

Thank God she had a better sense of timing than he did. What the hell was he thinking, bringing up someone from her past? But Jamal knew much of the battle he was fighting to win Phylicia over was due to what this guy had done to her. He wanted to know what he was up against.

Not tonight, though. They had better things to do tonight.

"Jamal, it's late," Phylicia said.

Or maybe not.

She pushed away from the counter she'd been leaning against and walked over to where he sat.

"I don't want to waste any more time dancing around the issue," she continued. "We're both adults. We can be upfront about what we want to happen here."

Desire shot to his groin. "I want you," he said without hesitation.

"I want you, too," she returned.

Damn. Her boldness turned him on more than Jamal thought possible. How hot was it to have a woman tell him just what she wanted? No teasing. No games.

Without another word he captured the back of her head and pulled her close. She met his mouth with eagerness that rivaled his own, her lips parting and her tongue darting inside his mouth.

Jamal opened his legs so she could step between them, then thought better of it. Why waste time being vertical?

"Where's your bed?" he asked.

Phylicia took him by the hand and led him down a short hallway. His mouth salivated at the way the jeans molded to her trim thighs. He needed to peel them off of her. Now.

They entered her bedroom, and Phylicia flipped on a bedside lamp.

"Okay. Strip," she said.

Jamal managed a hoarse laugh through the lust clogging his throat. "Is this going to be a game of Show Me Yours and I'll Show You Mine?"

"We don't have time for that," she said, then caught the hem of her blouse and pulled it over her head. Jamal's knees instantly weakened at the sight of her in a barely there sheer black bra.

"Damn," he whispered.

"Are you going to get undressed?" she asked.

"Hell, yes," he said, and kicked off his shoes.

It was an all-out strip fest from that point on. In a matter of seconds, they were both naked. Jamal wanted to take a few minutes to just look at her, but Phylicia was having none of that. She reached for him and pulled him down on the bed with her.

Jamal attacked her body with a full-on sensual assault. Sucking first one nipple into his mouth, then the other, snaking his hand down her rib cage and over her hip, rubbing her smooth inner thigh before slipping a finger into the soaking wetness between her legs. She lifted her hips, reaching for his touch. He answered by sliding another finger into her tight body.

"Dammit, Phylicia." She was so tight. So wet.

"More," she moaned against his lips, her body surging beneath him.

Jamal added another finger, gliding them in and out of her slippery, silken, scorching-hot passage. He escalated his pace and added his thumb to the action, circling around her swelling clitoris.

Phylicia closed her legs, impriso arm between her thighs.

"Faster," she breathed. "Go de looked up at him. "You. I need e me."

The erection he was certai get any harder swelled even mo lled a condom from his wal ickly covered himself before br en her thighs. He attempted to ea inside, but when Phylicia's hands grip his ass, all thoughts of gentleness evaporated. He plunged inside her, sinking into the most delicious warmth he'd ever invaded.

With single-minded determination, he drove into her, her body expanding to accommodate his increasingly deeper thrust.

It was heaven. Pure heaven. Jamal concentrated on the feel of her surrounding him, clutching him, milking him. He held himself still, relishing the snug fit.

Phylicia lifted her hips, seeking more, and he readily gave in to her demands, immersing himself in the soaking-wet sanctuary between her legs, over and over.

"Oh, God. You feel so good," she screamed, her fingernails digging into his back.

The painful glide of her nails coalesced with the pleasurable sensation of her tight, wet body closing around him. Jamal clutched her ass in his palms, holding her steady as he relentlessly drove deeper and deeper into her.

Phylicia clamped her hand behind his head and buried her face against his neck just as she exploded around him. Jamal felt her teeth graze his skin, and it sent him over the edge. He came hard and fast, his entire body trembling with the force of it.

He rolled over and collapsed on the bed, his chest hurting with the force of the breaths he was required to take.

"Oh, God," Phylicia said with a satisfied

sigh. "That was so much better than Bob."

Jamal pushed up on one elbow and pinned her with a dark glare. "Are you kidding me? You bring up your ex-boyfriend now?"

She let out a breathless laugh. "Bob isn't my ex-boyfriend. He's my vibrator," she said. "And you just put him to shame."

Jamal shook his head. "A woman who names her vibrator. Could I get any luckier?" A wicked smile broke out over his lips. "Actually, I think I can."

Phylicia peered up at him. With the sexiest smile known to mankind, she relaxed her legs and gestured toward the nightstand. "Bob's in the top drawer. Go for it."

No. He really could not be luckier.

CHAPTER 9

Even the swath of sunlight that traveled across her face, waking her up, couldn't erase the smile that tilted up the corners of Phil's mouth. A delicious ache throbbed between her legs. She smiled at that, too. It had been a long time since she'd experienced that kind of ache.

"God, I needed this." She sighed. Her body still hummed with the pleasure of being good and properly satisfied by a man who knew *exactly* what to do with the tools he'd been given. And those she'd purchased through an erotic online store.

She lifted her head and tilted it toward the bathroom, listening for running water or some other indication that Jamal was in there.

Nothing.

Phil pushed up from the bed and walked over to the bathroom. It was empty.

"He left?" she said with disbelief.

155

She unhooked her bathrobe from behind the door and wrapped it around her, tying the satin sash at her waist. When she went into the living area, she immediately noticed the door to the spare room off the kitchen slightly ajar.

A shimmer of disquiet rolled down her spine.

She stalked over to the door and threw it open. "What are you doing in here?" she asked.

Jamal whipped around. In his hands was the unframed canvas of the pond on the edge of Gauthier. She'd started the painting months ago but had not found the time to finish it yet.

"Are these your mom's?" he asked, nodding toward the nearly two dozen paintings leaning against the walls, all of them in various stages of completion.

Phil propped her shoulder against the doorjamb and crossed her arms in front of her. "They're mine," she answered.

His eyes widened. "Damn, Phylicia. What *can't* you do?" He looked back at the canvas in his hands. "How long have you been painting?"

"Most of my life," she said.

"These are . . ." He shook his head. "Amazing," he finally finished.

"That's Ponderosa Pond. Have you ever been?"

"No," he said. "But if it's half as nice as this painting, it's somewhere I definitely want to visit."

"Thank you," she said. His praise triggered a warmth that spread throughout her body. Phil was still unsure how she felt about his snooping around her house while she was asleep. Though, after the way she'd opened her body to him, he probably felt as if her home was open to him, as well.

"Do you want coffee?" she asked, moving away from the door and taking the painting out of his hand. She leaned it against the wall with the others and pulled him out of the room, closing the door behind him.

Jamal stopped their progress and stared down at her for several moments, his brow furrowed.

"Sorry if I intruded," he said. "I came upon the room by mistake. I was looking for a pantry because I was going to make coffee for *you*."

"It's okay." She tried to pull him farther into the kitchen.

He didn't budge. "I'm getting the sense that it really isn't."

Phil expelled a frustrated breath. "It's just that I haven't worked on any of that stuff in a really long time. Whenever I step into that room, it's a reminder that I've been neglecting my painting."

"Why did you stop? Too busy with your restoration work?"

If only . . .

"That's one of the reasons," she said.

"But when you're that good at something, you need to make the time."

"Really? So, before last night, when was the last time you'd played your sax?" she tossed back at him.

"Touché," he said, a grin pulling up the corner of his mouth. God, his mouth was gorgeous. And so very, very talented.

"However, since I did play last night, I think you should paint today," he reasoned.

"I will," Phil said. "I've got panels of wainscoting waiting for a fresh coat of paint. Why did you let me sleep so late? We should have been at the Victorian hours ago."

He shook his head. "We're not working on the house today." She started to protest, but he stopped her. "I just spoke to my contractor. His crew finished their previous job early, so they're starting on Belle Maison today. We can afford to take a day off."

"Since when?"

He leaned over and nibbled her ear. "Since I discovered the sounds you make when your friend Bob and I work together."

Phil's entire body blushed, just the mention of what he'd done to her last night heating her from the inside out.

"Come on, Phylicia. We can pack lunch and drive out to Ponderosa Pond. You can finish that painting."

"We can't," she said, but her protest lacked conviction.

The moist tip of his tongue traveled down her neck. "What will it take to convince you that we can?"

A shudder rolled through her body. "I'll get dressed," she said.

"I'm going to run to my place and get something more comfortable than the clothes I wore last night. I'll be back in fifteen minutes. Be ready."

A half hour later, Phil pointed to the dirt road off Highway 439. "Turn here," she told Jamal. He took a right, his shiny black truck kicking up dirt she saw in the rearview mirror.

"How much farther?" he asked.

"It's just beyond that curve."

They rounded the bend in the road and a small meadow opened up, the pond in the distance. The left side of the water was blocked by a copse of trees of varying heights.

"Who knew this little slice of paradise was hidden back here?" Jamal commented.

A curtain of vines hung from the branches of a huge oak tree that sat just at the edge of the pond. Tall reeds bowed to the will of the gentle breeze blowing across the pasture.

"It's a well-kept secret here in Gauthier," Phil said.

She collected her canvases and painting supplies from the back of Jamal's double-cab truck, while he carried the easel. She set up her painting area a few yards to the right, using the truck to block some of the breeze.

"Do you mind if I watch, or will it make you nervous?" Jamal asked.

She looked back at him. "I don't mind."

Within moments she was lost in her work. Jamal sat just beyond her shoulder, but it didn't bother her in the least as she rediscovered everything she loved about what used to be her favorite pastime.

Phil wasn't sure how much time had passed before she put the finishing touches on the tree.

"We need to move closer," she said. "When I started this painting, the reeds weren't this high. I want to make sure I get the water right."

They moved closer to the pond, setting

up shop just outside the drooping vines hanging from the oak tree. Phil dabbed touches of gold onto the canvas to reflect the sun's rays on the water.

She turned back to find Jamal lounging in the grass underneath the tree branches, his elbows bent, his legs crossed at the ankles. He looked incredibly sexy, his leanly muscled body stretched out the way it was. A work of art.

"You look as if you're posing for me," Phil said.

"Have you ever painted a human subject?"

She shook her head. "Just landscapes."

"I thought all true artists had to master the human form in its natural state?"

Her mouth dried up. She swallowed hard, unable to stop herself from licking her lips. "I guess I can't call myself a true artist," she said. "I've never had the opportunity to paint the human form in its natural state."

Jamal's brow peaked. "You want it?"

"You offering?"

"Depends." He stood and toed off his shoes, kicking them a few feet away.

Phil pulled her bottom lip between her teeth. "On what?"

Jamal's eyes traveled the length of her body, the makings of a smile pulling at the corners of his mouth. "What I get in return," he said. He caught the hem of his shirt.

"We can, uh, figure out a modeling fee," she said, her voice slightly dazed as she watched him pull the shirt over his head. "Maybe I'll shave some of the price off of my bill for the work I'm doing at Belle Maison."

An entirely too wicked grin broke out on his face. He unzipped his shorts and pulled them, along with his boxers, down his legs.

"I think we can come up with something better than that."

Phil tried to close her mouth, but it didn't work. A nude man should seem out of place in their surroundings, but Jamal looked as if he was right where he belonged. She'd spent the night in close quarters with his naked body, but this was her first chance to actually *see* him.

Magnificent didn't even come close. He was just the way she liked her men — lean, but sculpted with tight, defined muscles. Even though he had given up baseball years ago, he still had an athlete's body.

"Where do you want me?" Jamal asked.

"That's a loaded question," she answered, and he let out a sharp laugh. "Are you serious about this?" Phil asked.

He spread his arms wide. "What do you think?"

Another loaded question.

She couldn't describe what she was thinking right now. That he was too sinfully put together for words? That she wanted him to sprawl out on the grass so she could lick him from head to toe? That she wanted to strip out of her clothes and join him?

"Assume the pose you had before you undressed," she said, grateful she'd snatched a blank canvas before leaving the house. She removed the painting she'd been working on from the easel and replaced it with the blank one.

Jamal lowered himself to the ground and stretched out again. For several moments Phil just stared at the picture he created. His abs were ripped like a proverbial washboard. Those legs sculpted with powerful, lean muscles. His very generous male parts thick and resting against his inner thigh.

Lickable. So, so lickable.

"I'm not sure where to start," Phil murmured.

"Start with whatever catches your eye," Jamal said.

She looked at him over the canvas and couldn't help but laugh. Reining in the nervous, giddy flutters floating around her stomach, she called on the serious artist she knew was hidden somewhere within her and got to work.

Looking at him through a painter's eye, she caressed the canvas with the charcoal, mimicking the long lines of his sinewy torso. She captured their surroundings, sketching the base of the huge oak tree, imagining how she would bring the painting to life with the brilliant greens and soft browns.

Twenty minutes later, Phil had the sketch complete. "I think I'm done," she said.

"Really? That was fast." He pushed up from the ground and strode over to her. Coming around the easel, he said over her shoulder, "You *sure* you're done?"

"It's not *finished* finished. It's just the outline," she said. She picked up the brush. "Now I have to flesh it out with the actual paint."

A strong arm looped around her waist. "Speaking of flesh . . . I seem to be the only one showing some here," Jamal murmured against her neck.

"Hey, you're the one who offered to strip."

"I think you should return the favor."

"I know you don't think you're gonna get me to strip out here," she said.

"You wanna bet?" he asked and snaked a hand inside her shirt.

Phil disengaged from his hold and side-stepped him. "Keep back," she warned, holding him off with her paintbrush.

"Or what?"

"Don't try me," she said.

He took a step forward, and she brandished the brush like a saber. When he took a second step, Phil lashed out with the brush, sweeping a stroke of green paint across his pectorals.

Jamal's eyes darted down at his chest and then back up at her. "I can't believe you did that," he said.

"I warned you," Phil said, a giggle bubbling up in her throat.

"Oh, you're in for it."

Phil let out a yelp as he dived for her. She scuttled around the meadow, still wielding her paintbrush in his direction. She made a full circle before Jamal caught up with her, back underneath the tree. He wrapped both arms around her, imprisoning her in his strong embrace.

"Stop it." She laughed. "I told you to stay back." She managed to swipe another swath of green, this time on his arm.

Jamal tightened his hold, locking her against his hard body. "If you wanted to use my body as a canvas, all you had to do was ask," he whispered into her ear.

His suggestion shot a naughty tremor down her spine. Phil glanced back at him over her shoulder.

"Really?" she asked.

That sexier-than-sin smile curved up the corners of his mouth. Jamal released her and walked over to the easel. Retrieving the palette, he sauntered back to where she stood and held it out to her.

Phil took it from him and looked on in mute fascination as he reclined on the patch of flattened grass where he'd lounged earlier.

"Well?" he said, one brow spiked in cocky challenge.

Palette in one hand and brush in the other, Phil dropped to her knees.

"What do you want me to paint?" she asked, the brush hovering just above his shoulder.

Jamal cocked his head to the side. "You know what? I've changed my mind." He sat up and plucked the palette and brush from her hands. "It's my turn to paint. Strip."

Phil regarded him with a stern frown. "I told you I was not getting naked."

"Strip," he said again.

The force of that single word, combined with all the sexy implications that accompanied it, sent a rush of heat skittering across her skin.

Was she really going to do this?

Apparently so. Despite the apprehension that threaded through her bloodstream, Phil took off her shirt and unsnapped her shorts.

"That's it," Jamal encouraged.

"I cannot believe I'm doing this," she said as she lifted her hips and drew the shorts over them. Moments later she lay before him in her hot pink bikini-cut cotton panties and matching bra.

"Am I wearing underwear?" he asked. "As sexy as that looks on you, you need to take off the rest."

Goose bumps traveled up and down her arms, but Phil obeyed, reaching behind her back and unhooking the bra's single eye-hook. She hunched over slightly and let it fall from her chest, the soft cotton causing her overly stimulated skin to pebble as it slid down her arms.

She heard the deep breath Jamal sucked in. He nodded, his gaze centered on her breasts.

"The last piece," he ordered.

Phil lifted her hips again and pulled her panties down her legs, tossing them next to her bra. "You happy now?" she asked.

"You'll know just how much in a minute," he said.

Her eyes drifted to his lap, where the evidence of his happiness was gradually swelling. He knelt next to her and said, "Lie back."

Dipping the brush in the paint, he trailed a line of sky blue down the valley between her breasts. It traveled along her stomach, causing her belly to tremble involuntarily. Jamal circled the tip of the brush around her belly button before continuing down, stopping at the neatly trimmed thatch of hair.

He pulled his lower lip between his teeth as he seemed to contemplate his next move. He added more paint to the brush and returned to her upper body, looping the brush around the base of her right breast.

Her eyes fluttered closed as Jamal lowered his head and pulled her puckered nipple into his mouth. Phil let out a soft moan, her back arching at the contact to her sensitized skin.

He repeated the process on the other breast, drawing a circle around the base before dipping his head and laving her with his tongue. His teeth grazed her nipple, then he sucked it into his mouth, tugging with a delicious pull that shot straight to the spot between her legs.

"More," she said. She felt his rumble of

laughter vibrate across her skin.

"You just love issuing orders, don't you?"

"What?" Phil asked, her forehead creasing in a quizzical frown.

"More. Harder. Deeper. You were like a drill sergeant last night."

Her entire body flushed with embarrassment. "Did I really say those things?"

He nodded. "I think it's sexy."

She smiled up at him. "Well, get to work," she ordered.

Jamal set the brush and palette on the grass and climbed over her. Hovering above her on all fours, he returned his attention to her breasts, stroking the tips with his tongue. He brushed his lips down her right side, peppering her ribs with kisses, nipping her hip with a gentle love bite. He moved lower, capturing her knees and pushing them apart.

Phil's stomach pulled tight as the spot between her legs pulsed with anticipation. Lifting herself up on her elbows, she peered down as Jamal's head lowered between her legs. She let out a small cry at the first wet swipe of his tongue. With unforgiving relentlessness he worked his tongue up and down, pleasuring her with every decadent stroke. He swirled the tip around her clitoris, flicking in rapid succession before drawing it between his lips.

Phil clutched his head in her hands and cried up at the sky, lifting her lower body off the ground and giving herself over to his demanding tongue. Tremors racked her body as the orgasm that had been building erupted.

She fell limply back into the trampled grass, her limbs relaxing in satisfied relief. The butterflies in her belly started swarming again as Jamal traveled back up her body, dropping light kisses along her torso. He hovered over her, smears of blue paint tracking across his chest from where he'd rubbed against her.

"What does the drill sergeant want me to do next?" he asked.

Phil contemplated his question for a moment before saying, "Lie down."

He complied, mirroring her pose in the grass. Phil summoned the strength to push herself up. She reached for the brush and palette, but Jamal caught her arm and shook his head.

"I think we've done enough painting for today," he said.

"What is it you want me to do then?"

The gleam in his eye told her exactly what he wanted.

Nervous excitement trembled low in her

belly. There were certain things she didn't do with a man unless she trusted him implicitly. She wasn't sure when she'd began to trust Jamal, but she did. And she wanted to do this for him.

He rose on one elbow and cradled her cheek in his palm. "You don't have to if you don't want to, Phylicia."

She captured his hand and removed it from her face, brushing her lips across the back of his fingers. Then, with a hand to his chest, she ushered him back onto the grass.

Jamal's eyelids lowered halfway and a slightly dazed look came over his face as she straddled his lower legs. Phil licked her lips before she bent over and pulled his thickening erection into her mouth. She heard his swift intake of breath, felt the shudder that quaked through him.

With unhurried movements, she worked her mouth up and down the length of him, running her tongue along the ridge of skin that rimmed the head, licking the spurt of precome that dripped from the tip. She relaxed her jaws so she could open wider, lowering her head until he hit the back of her throat, then sucking hard as she glided her mouth back up.

Jamal's hand cupped her head as he guided her up and down. His eyes shut

171

tight, he pitched his head back, his groans echoing around the vacant meadow.

"Phylicia," he said with a strained whisper.

Phil drew him into her mouth over and over again, giving extra attention to the smooth head, wrapping her tongue around it. She sensed his balls drawing tight and, moments later, felt the rush of salty liquid hit the back of her throat as he erupted in her mouth.

"Damn," Jamal breathed. He pulled in several deep breaths, his chest rising and falling. "That was a hell of a lot better than watching you paint."

Phil grinned as she enclosed his softening erection in her palm. She glided her hand up and down his smooth length, a heady sense of power building within her as she felt it grow hard again.

She lowered her head to take him into her mouth once more, but Jamal stopped her.

"No," he said. "In my pocket. There's a condom in my wallet."

Phil reached for the shorts he'd shucked off earlier and tore the wallet from the back pocket. She opened it and pulled out a condom. Tearing the packet open with her teeth, she rolled the latex down his now-stiff erection, her hands shaking. She straddled his hips, and like a woman desper-

172

ate for her next breath, sank onto him.

Jamal cradled her waist, guiding her up and down. Phil splayed her palms flat over his muscled chest and gripped, trying to find purchase on top of him. With fevered pumping, she rode him hard, her entire being erupting in a swift, pleasure-soaked orgasm that tore a scream from her throat and sent her crashing down on top of him.

They lay in the grass completely spent, their ragged breathing the only sound around them.

Jamal trailed his finger in a gentle caress along Phylicia's arm, starting from her shoulder and ending at her wrist. He couldn't stop touching her, not as if he'd tried. If he had it his way, he'd take her back to his house and spend the next week gaining intimate knowledge of every delicious inch of her body.

"Which room was yours?" he asked her.

He'd spent the past hour learning more about her years growing up at Belle Maison. He'd never seen her more open and animated as she talked about her childhood there. But there was also a trace of sadness that lingered over her words, a forlornness that made him ache for her.

"I had the upstairs room that overlooks

173

the front lawn, though I slept in the one with the balcony during the fall. I loved sleeping with the French doors open because of the breeze and the sound of the cicadas."

"That's why you wanted to make love out here. You like the sounds of nature."

"May I remind you that *you* are the one who initiated that?" she asked.

"Because I could tell how much you wanted it," he teased, nipping her shoulder.

"You are so cocky." She laughed. "Anyway, I just want to make sure you appreciate that house. It was a special place to grow up."

"What happened, Phylicia? Why did you sell it?" Jamal wasn't surprised when he felt her stiffen against him. "I know you don't want to talk about it," he said. "But I'm asking you to anyway."

She let out an audible breath and tilted her head to the side, resting it against his shoulder. "I put the house up as collateral for a loan I took out last year," she said. "Me and . . . a business partner went in on a house-flipping venture. I bought three foreclosed houses in Maplesville for a pretty good deal and renovated them, but the housing market tanked and the houses have been on the market ever since.

"When I couldn't make the payments on

the construction loan, the bank repossessed Belle Maison."

"Dammit," Jamal said. "I figured you'd lost it, but I couldn't figure out how."

"Well, I haven't really shared the details with anyone. Not even Mya."

"What about this business partner?" he asked, though Jamal had a feeling he already knew who — and what — the business partner was to her.

"He's a coward who I thought I was in love with," she said matter-of-factly. "When the going got tough, he skipped town. The loan was in my name, so he got off scot-free."

"What's his name?" Jamal asked, his anger rising so swiftly it shocked him.

"Doesn't even matter," she said. "He's inconsequential."

"Did he talk you into buying the houses?"

"It was originally his idea, but I went along with it one hundred percent," she said. "I allowed myself to fall into that situation. I've stopped blaming Kevin."

"Kevin," Jamal spat. "I never liked that name."

She let out a sad laugh. "I certainly don't like it now."

"Have you been able to dig yourself out of the hole?" he asked.

She shook her head. "I'm trying, but it's not as if I get a steady paycheck, you know? And with the mortgage on my house, and the cost of my mom's care facility going up—"

"What about your mom?"

She leaned her head back and closed her eyes. "Oh, gosh," she said on a weary breath. "My mouth is like a faucet I can't turn off." She looked at him and shook her head. "Jamal, the last thing I want to do right now is unload all my problems on you."

"I'm asking you to," he said. "What about your mom?"

"My mother suffers from early-onset dementia. She lives in a facility in Slidell that specializes in dementia patients. It's extremely expensive, but it's one of the best. I foot the bill for what Medicaid and my dad's life insurance policy don't cover."

"So you're taking care of two households," he said.

"Basically." She nodded.

"And trying to pay off a loan and three additional mortgages?"

"Those other three houses don't have mortgages, thank goodness. But they're still not creating revenue, and I still have to pay property taxes on them. My finances are what Mya would call a hot mess."

He hesitated for a moment, already anticipating what her reaction would be. But he couldn't *not* make the suggestion. "Phylicia, don't take this the wrong way, but I want —"

"Don't even think of offering me money," she said, pushing away from him and turning to face him. "I didn't tell you any of this to get money out of you. I didn't even *want* to tell you any of this."

"I know you aren't trying to get money out of me. I'm offering it."

"No," she said.

"Phylicia, I can afford it," he said. "Even if you insist on paying me back, at least you can save on the interest."

"Jamal, are you insane?" she asked. "*If* I insist on paying you back? Even if I were to accept money from you — which I would not — do you think I would just take it without paying it back?"

"I'm just putting it out there as an option, Phylicia."

"We hardly know each other," she reasoned.

His head reared back, her words knocking the air from his lungs.

"Okay, I know what we did just a little while ago contradicts that, but let's be honest here, Jamal. The fact is we really *don't* know each other all that well," she reiterated. "My financial problems have nothing to do with you. I got myself into this mess, and I'll eventually get myself out." She shook her head again. "I can't believe I even told you about this."

"As you pointed out, you didn't want to tell me. I asked," he reminded her. He reached for her, rubbing her thigh. "Look, I don't want this to ruin our afternoon together."

Though, from the dour look on her face, it was evident that it already had. Dammit, why couldn't he just leave well enough alone?

Because he knew something was troubling her, and he had needed to know what it was. He hated to see the distress clouding her eyes.

She looked up at him, those brown eyes filled with apology. "I'm sorry," she said. "Leave it to me to bite someone's head off for offering to help me out."

"It's okay, Phylicia."

"No, it's ungracious and totally goes against my southern roots," she said with just enough Scarlett O'Hara twang to draw a smile from him. Her expression became serious once again as she caressed his cheek.

"It really was sweet of you, but it's not your problem, Jamal. It's mine, and I'll eventually find a way out of it. I'll just overcharge you for the work I'm doing on the house."

He grinned at her quip, but he ached to fix this for her. He knew that money was not a cure-all, but in this situation, it was. He could easily write her a check and take care of all the things causing her distress.

"This kind of put a downer on the day, didn't it?" she said. She looked up at him, her eyes bright. "We could have sex again. It'll lighten things up."

He did laugh this time. "I only had that one condom with me."

"I noticed that," she said. "You weren't feeling very confident in your powers of persuasion, were you?"

"I figured after using three last night, neither of us would be able to handle more than one time today."

"It's been a long time since I did this, buddy. I can handle a whole lot."

"That's all you had to say. We'll stop in at the pharmacy on our way back. I'll make sure to stock up."

"You do that and talk of our torrid love affair will be all over town before sunset."

"Is that what we're having?" Jamal asked. "A torrid love affair?"

She leaned over him, her face hovering mere centimeters from his. "Actually, we're having an *inappropriate,* torrid love affair. I'm technically your employee. If we were working in Corporate America, I could file a sexual harassment lawsuit against you."

"But you wouldn't," he said, threading his fingers through her hair and palming the back of her head.

"Probably not," she said, lowering herself on top of him. "If I filed suit against you, we'd have to stop doing this."

"And why in the hell would we do that?" Jamal said before touching his mouth to hers.

CHAPTER 10

Phil leaned her head against the leather headrest and closed her eyes, letting the gentle bumps in the dirt road lull her. She was trying frantically not to panic at the thought of everything she'd let slip with Jamal.

Let slip?

Yeah, right. She was like a damn guest on a talk show, broadcasting her business to the world.

What on earth had possessed her to run off at the mouth? The only people who knew about her bad business deal with Kevin were the coward himself and a couple of faceless people at the bank. She hadn't confided in anyone else — not even her best friend. Yet she'd shared everything with Jamal?

It was the sex. That had to be it. Give her just a little action down there and she lost all of her common sense.

Well, she hadn't lost *all* of her common sense. She'd had enough to refuse his offer of money.

Phil still could not believe he'd suggested it. They barely knew each other. She could take his money and leave him high and dry, skip out to California just as Kevin had done to her. Of course, she'd never leave her mother, but Jamal didn't know that.

Even as she applauded herself for rightly refusing his offer, Phil let herself imagine, just for a moment, how it would have felt to take him up on it. Having the burden of all her financial worries eliminated just by uttering a simple *yes*.

"Why are you so quiet?" Jamal asked.

Phil jumped slightly and lolled her head toward him. "Just recuperating from the last hour," she said.

"Sorry about that," he said, his grin wicked. "But with no condoms left, that was the only way I could think to satisfy you."

"Mission accomplished." Phil laughed.

"If you didn't insist on going back to work on the house, we could do a whole lot more of that, all afternoon and into the night."

"We're on a timetable, remember?" she said. "I need to bring the crown molding in the downstairs parlor to my shop. I want to see how closely I can match those pieces we picked up at the salvage yard. If you want to, you can come over to my place and watch me work."

"You know how much I love watching you work," he said. "And that goes for more than just what you're doing on the house."

Phil rolled her eyes.

She should have known they would fall into this light, easy banter; it had been this way the night of Mya and Corey's wedding. Even though she'd kept the conversation purposely superficial — talking about hot news items, movies they'd seen, books they'd read and other things that usually encompassed first-date conversation — she'd sensed that finding something to say to Jamal would never be all that hard.

Phil had discovered that *talking* to him wasn't the only easy thing to do. She'd never in her life fallen into bed with a man so quickly, let alone completely dispelling her inhibitions and allowing him to do all the things he'd done — and the things she'd done to him.

She stopped just short of licking her lips. She could still feel his silky hardness against her tongue, taste his deep, musky flavor. She was dying to taste him again.

Without warning, acute panic tightened her chest.

Was she setting herself up for heartache? She knew better than to lose her head over a man. Wasn't she still paying the high price of falling in love once before?

But this wasn't love. This was lust.

Phil glanced over at his strong profile, at the powerful jaw and those incredibly talented lips.

Oh, yeah. She was in serious lust with this man.

His eyes on the road, Jamal said, "Unless you want me to pull the truck over, you may want to stop looking at me like that." He glanced at her. "It's an option, you know. The windows are tinted. No one will see what's going on inside."

"Just drive," Phil said. "I think I can control myself until we get to an actual bed."

"You're stronger than I am," he said. "I've had to stop myself at least five times from finding a tree to park the truck behind so I can have at you again."

Goose bumps traveled across her skin at the image that popped into her head. At this point, Phil was happy to get any man who was willing to provide a bit of sexual relief. To find one who was a downright master at it was better than winning the lottery.

She made a show of leaning over and peering at the speedometer. "Can't you drive any faster?"

Jamal's deep chuckle resonated within the truck's cab. A few minutes later they turned onto Loring Avenue. Phil almost suggested that he park in the back of the house so they could make use of the truck's ample cab room. It had to be more comfortable than going at it on the Victorian's bare floors, and she wasn't sure she could wait until they drove to her house and her comfortable bed.

"I'm giving us five minutes to load the molding into the truck," Jamal issued. "Whatever doesn't get in there doesn't get done. And you're not touching them until after I've had you at least twice."

"Are you expecting a complaint?" Phil asked.

"God, how I love an insatiable woman," he said.

They turned into the graveled driveway at Belle Maison, and Phil felt the blood drain from her face. A whimper of alarm climbed from her throat, and her entire body went cold at the sight of a huge backhoe tractor shoving its metal claws into the heart of her mother's painting room.

"Dammit," Jamal whispered as he slowed the truck to a stop.

Phil opened the door and sprang from the

truck, rushing over to the side of the house where the room was located. She waved her hands over her head, trying to catch the driver's attention, but to no avail. The claws impaled another section of the room, taking out a side wall and two of the huge windows.

"Shit," she heard Jamal say as he came around the house. He ran over to the tractor and climbed the side of the moving vehicle, banging on the window. The machine screeched to a halt and the driver pulled off the earmuffs covering his ears.

Phil could hear the two talking, but she didn't try to make out what they were saying. What did it matter? The damage had been done. Half of her mother's room lay in rubble. Phil wrapped her arms around her stomach in an attempt to stave off the rush of grief threatening to overwhelm her.

"Stop it," she ordered herself.

Straightening her back, she steeled herself against the emotion clogging her throat and banished the tears that had attempted to collect in the corners of her eyes. She would not cry. After everything she'd been through these past few years, she would not let her emotions run away with her.

Jamal climbed down from the tractor and started toward her. The sorrow clouding his face brought Phil a measure of comfort . . .

but only a small measure.

"Phylicia, I am so sorry about this," he said. "I was supposed to cancel the wrecking service, but with everything that was going on, it just slipped my mind."

She gave him a sharp nod, not fully trusting herself to speak. Not fully trusting him, either. What if he'd never intended to save the room? What if he'd only made that promise in order to get her to continue working on the house?

Her gut told her Jamal would never do that, but she had relied on her gut with Kevin, and he'd proved to be the exact opposite of the man she thought he was. The same could be true of Jamal. She just didn't know.

And wasn't that the truth smacking her in the face?

Reality washed over her like a tidal wave, bombarding her with a truth that was hard to swallow. This man was more of a stranger to her than ninety percent of the population of this town. But because it had made it easier to share her body with him, she'd created a false sense of familiarity.

Wrapping her arms around her upper body, Phil swallowed past the lump that had formed in her throat.

It was time to leave this dream world she'd

been immersed in for the past thirty-six hours. Jamal Johnson was her employer. She'd allowed him to become her lover — a mistake she would no doubt pay dearly for.

Get over it, Phil ordered herself.

"Let's load the crown molding into the truck," she said, turning on her heel and heading for the front entry, where she'd stacked the molding yesterday.

"Phylicia, wait." He grabbed her by the elbow, halting her steps.

Phil pulled her arm out of his grip and turned to him. She ached to lash out at him, but she quelled the impulse. Employees had no right to be insubordinate to their employers.

"Yes?" she asked in the calmest voice she could muster.

"I'm sorry about the room," he said.

"This is your house, Jamal. You don't have to apologize for anything."

His head reared back, his eyes narrowing into slits. "You don't believe me, do you?" he asked with a measure of suspicion.

"It doesn't matter what I believe," she said, still calm. Score one for her.

"The hell it doesn't," he argued. "I'm telling you the truth, Phylicia. I was supposed to call the wrecking service when I left your house last Monday, but I got sidetracked. I forgot to call."

"You don't have to explain it to me. This is *your* house," she reiterated. "I have no say in what happens to it. Now, can we please load the molding into the truck so I can get it back to my shop? We've lost too much time over the past day and a half. I have a lot of work to make up for."

Jamal's eyes slid shut. He brought his hand up to knead the bridge of his nose. "Phylicia, don't do this," he said in a pained voice.

"Once we get everything loaded, I'll need you to drive me home," was all she said.

Twenty minutes later, they were pulling into her driveway. Phil grabbed her keys from the front compartment of the bag that held her painting supplies. She entered through the side door of her workshop and then raised the garage door from the inside. She cleared off a spot on one of her worktables.

She looked over at Jamal's truck to find him still sitting behind the wheel, staring at her with that brooding look he'd had for the past twenty minutes. He opened the door and got out, shutting it with more force than necessary.

They hadn't said a word to each other since she'd left him standing in the yard at

Belle Maison.

Phil went around the back of the truck and reached for a strip of molding.

"I've got them," Jamal said. He pulled out an armful of the long wooden pieces and carried it into the garage.

Well, she was not going to just stand here and watch him do all the work.

Jamal eyed her as she carted several strips of molding into the garage. He carried the remaining pieces in and stacked them with the others, then he turned to her, his expression still dark with anger.

"I apologized for the room, Phylicia. What else do you want me to do? Rebuild it?"

The fact that her father had built the room for her mother made it special. His rebuilding it would mean nothing.

"I don't want you to do anything, Jamal, and that includes apologizing. I already told you, you have nothing to apologize for. It's your house."

"You've pointed that out already. Stop pretending as if that's the only thing that matters here."

"It *is* all that matters," Phil said. "You hired me to work on the house. I'd lost sight of that. What happened today reminded me of what my objective is."

He shook his head. "I can't believe this."

He stared at her, accusation and anger heavy in his eyes. "So, what does this mean, Phylicia? Does this mean I'm getting in my truck and going home?"

Phil swallowed a hard knot of emotion and nodded. "I have work to do."

The fury emanating from Jamal was a living, breathing thing. He stared at her for so long; it took everything Phil had in her not to flinch under his glare. She waited for him to blast her with another accusation, but after several more uncomfortably long moments, he turned and stalked back to his truck. He yanked the door open and climbed in, revving the engine and peeling out of her driveway like someone trying to win a drag race.

Phil had to take several deep breaths before she could even think of moving from the spot where she stood.

She'd let it happen again. She had allowed herself to get caught up in the romance of good sex and good conversation, knowing all it would do was muddle her brain and make her lose sight of her real agenda.

At least this time she'd reined it in before things got too far out of control.

Right. As if rolling around in the grass while letting the man have his way with her naked body was anywhere *near* being in control of the situation.

"Lesson learned," Phil murmured. "Again," she tacked on with an annoyed snort.

But this time the lesson would stick.

Jamal stared at his cell phone for a solid minute as he watched the time switch from 9:59 to 10:00 a.m. Phylicia was two hours late, which probably meant that she wasn't going to show up at all.

Probably?

From the minute he'd sped out of her driveway, something in his gut told him this would happen. She was going to quit working on the house, would probably avoid him like the plague whenever she passed him around town. How in the hell did he go from licking every part of the woman's body to this?

Jamal cast a derisive glance at the spot where her mother's painting room once stood.

What else could he do to convince Phylicia that tearing the room down had been one humongous mistake? Probably nothing. From the way things had ended between them yesterday, Jamal wasn't sure if he should even try.

"Damn that," he bit out.

He tossed the miter saw onto his work-table and shut off his iPod. He didn't even bother telling the work crew that he was leaving. He just climbed into his truck and took off, his mind's focus on one thing.

He pulled into Phylicia's driveway, having a hard time recalling a minute of the fifteen-minute drive that brought him here. Her blue pickup truck was parked where it had been yesterday, which meant she was probably home. Jamal went to the front door and rang the doorbell, but after a couple of minutes with no answer, he headed for her workshop.

The door was unlocked, as usual. He entered and immediately spotted her toward the rear of the room, her back to him. She stood before a huge armoire, sliding the flat end of a putty knife up the front of it.

Wynton Marsalis streamed through her CD player. Jamal's gut clenched at the memory of that song playing just two nights ago as they'd made love in her bed. He stopped a few feet behind her and waited until she'd stripped a smooth, uniform band of old varnish from the armoire before tapping her on the shoulder.

She gasped and turned, the putty knife slipping from her fingers.

"Good God." She covered her chest with

both hands. "What is it with you sneaking up on me?"

"Why didn't you show up this morning?" Jamal asked.

She jutted her chin in the air. "Professional emergency," she answered. "The guy who owns this called me last night and asked if I could get it done right away. He found a buyer for it. He agreed to pay an extra twenty percent for the rush job. I couldn't pass it up."

"And it didn't occur to you to call and let me know you wouldn't be working at Belle Maison today?"

She shrugged. "Guess I forgot. You know how that is, don't you?"

His entire body tensed. He forced himself to swallow the temper that flared at her flippant jab.

"I'm sorry," Phylicia said with a slight grimace. "That was uncalled for. I'm usually not this petty. And definitely not this unprofessional."

He didn't want her apology; he just wanted to know where they stood.

"Be straight with me, Phylicia. Are you pulling out of the job?" Jamal asked, his chest tightening painfully as he anticipated her answer.

"No," she said. "I agreed to work on the

house." She stooped to pick up the putty knife that had fallen when he'd startled her, then stood and faced him again. "However, I am requesting a couple of days off so I can get this armoire done. I usually wouldn't leave in the middle of one job to work on another, but this antiques dealer is new to the area. If I can make a good impression on this job, there's potential for more work."

Jamal crossed his arms over his chest. "And you're not going to just find another project to work on after you're done with the armoire?"

"No," she stated. "That's not how I operate. And frankly, I need the money you're paying me."

"So that's the only reason you're staying on?" he asked. "Because of the money?"

She looked up at him, the indifference in her expression slicing through him. "Isn't that why we all work?" she asked.

"Not everyone."

"Unlike some people, I don't have the luxury of picking and choosing when I want to work. Now, do you have a problem with me taking a few days off?"

"What if I do?" he challenged.

Her lips thinned into a tight, angry line. "Then I guess I'll have to tell my other client that he'll have to wait. I don't want word getting out that Phillips' Home Restoration doesn't complete a job. My reputation is everything to me."

Jamal nearly choked on the anger climbing up his throat. "You know I would never say anything to hurt your business," he bit out.

"You also said you wouldn't tear down my mother's room. I'm not sure I'm willing to risk my professional reputation on your word."

Jamal clamped down on the retort that nearly spewed from his mouth. He couldn't trust himself to speak.

Then again, there was nothing left to say. The damage was done, and likely irreparable.

He stared at her for several long moments, his chest developing a painful ache as she stared back with more animosity in her brown eyes than he'd ever been subjected to. Maybe her staying away for a few days was a good thing. He couldn't take her looking at him with such bitter resentment.

"Finish your armoire," he said. "I can take care of the Victorian."

She didn't say anything else. Just nodded and turned back to the piece of furniture.

Jamal stood in the shop several moments longer, deciding whether he should apologize yet again. But what had his previous apologies gotten him but more of her extremely cold shoulder? She was still too raw. Maybe after a few days, after she'd had time to move past her anger over the room, he could get her to see reason.

CHAPTER 11

For the next two days Jamal poured everything he had into working on the B&B. He arrived at Belle Maison an hour earlier than usual and stayed well after the contractors departed. By the end of the day he was too exhausted to do anything but shower and fall into a deep, dreamless sleep.

The quicker he got the work done on the house, the less time he'd have to deal with Phylicia's stony attitude when she returned. *If* she returned. He fully expected her to come up with another excuse to stay away.

He was installing the new fixtures in the downstairs bathroom when he heard a truck pulling into the driveway. He was instantly ashamed for thinking she would back out of the job. When it came to her work, Phylicia kept her word.

He was the one who hadn't. But, dammit, it wasn't his fault!

Jamal walked out onto the porch to find

Phylicia getting her tools out of the back of her truck. He'd try for a bit of civility; maybe then he could smooth things over and regain some ground with her.

"Good morning," Jamal said.

"Good morning," she answered, and moved right past him.

Jamal closed his eyes and let his chin fall to his chest. *So much for that.*

The rest of the day inched by in an excruciating stretch of long hours that were peppered with awkward silences and the occasional monosyllabic response whenever he asked her a question. The only time she spoke more than one word to him was when he asked her if she wanted to stop for lunch.

"I didn't bring my lunch with me," she told him.

"You want to go to Jessie's? My treat," Jamal offered.

"No, thanks. I'll just go home." She turned away from him and went back to work. Twenty minutes later, she climbed into her pickup truck and left him to eat alone.

Jamal sat on his truck's lowered tailgate, eating the ham sandwich he'd packed. He tried not to think of the lunches he and Phylicia had shared in this very spot, but that was like asking the sun not to come up.

He thought about her constantly. But it was the things they had done together sans clothing that occupied his mind more than anything else.

"Damn, this is messed up," Jamal said. He forced himself to swallow several more bites of his sandwich, purely for sustenance. His appetite had been nonexistent these past couple of days.

He couldn't go on like this much longer. Something had to give.

Maybe once they were no longer occupying the same uncomfortable space his life could regain a semblance of normalcy. With that goal in mind, Jamal gathered the remnants of his lunch and headed for the house. The sooner the bed-and-breakfast was finished, the better off he'd be. He cranked up the volume on his iPod speaker deck and returned to working on the downstairs bathroom.

He heard Phylicia's truck pull into the driveway, but he didn't bother to acknowledge her return from lunch. He had his work; she had hers. If this was how she wanted it, they could get their jobs done without speaking for the duration of this project.

Using her smallest chisel, Phil carved the

dirt that had built up in the crevices of the ornately carved banister with painstaking gentleness. This would be, by far, the most time-consuming aspect of her work on the Victorian, and unlike the wainscoting, unfortunately, it was immovable.

Over the past three weeks, she'd hauled whatever she could back to her workshop, preferring to work there instead of suffering under the weight of Jamal's brooding stares. The air between them was thick with tension, the silences louder than she could have ever thought possible.

Phil had come to the conclusion that the destruction of her mother's painting room had, more than likely, been a mistake. But it didn't change anything between them. Jamal was, first and foremost, a client. Getting involved with him had been foolhardy and dangerous. She was a professional, and professionals could not make such colossal errors in judgment if they wanted their businesses to succeed.

Of course, if she was a *real* professional, she never would have put herself in such an awkward work situation in the first place.

Phil heard the footsteps seconds before Jamal arrived in the foyer. She studied him through the slim balusters of the banister from her vantage point at the top of the stairs. His shoulders were rigid, as they had been for the past few weeks. Neither of them had been able to relax much.

She watched him lay out his tools on the floor, then drop to his haunches to shuffle through them.

Despite all the reasons she shouldn't, she had the strongest urge to walk downstairs, wrap her arms around his waist and beg him to come home with her right now. She missed the banter they shared. She missed the feel of his naked skin against hers.

"You are pathetic," she whispered.

Her cell phone rang, startling her. Jamal's head turned sharply, and he caught her staring down at him. Phil quickly pulled back from the banister, her phone nearly falling out of her hands as she clumsily pulled it from her pocket.

"Hello," she answered in a rushed breath.

As the person on the other side of the line spoke, Phil felt the blood drain from her face.

"I'll be right there," she said. Dropping everything, she raced down the stairs. "I have to go," she called over her shoulder as she jerked open the front door.

"Wait! What's going on?" Jamal grabbed her by the arm. "What's wrong?"

"It was Mossy Oaks. There's been some

type of incident with my mom. I need to get over there." Phil realized she was shaking from head to toe, but she couldn't help it.

"I'll come with you," Jamal said.

She shook her head. "No, that's okay."

"You're not driving like this, Phylicia. Don't waste time arguing with me."

"Fine," Phil said. "Hurry."

While he closed and locked the front door, Phil ran to her truck, cranking over the ignition with a violent turn.

"Move to the other side," Jamal said, opening the driver's side door.

She started to protest again, but Phil knew he was right. Her shaking hands would probably steer them clear off the road if she tried to drive. She scooted over to the passenger side and leaned her head back against the headrest as Jamal backed out of the driveway. She closed her eyes and concentrated on taking deep breaths as they headed south on Highway 21 toward Slidell.

"What did the person on the phone say?" Jamal asked.

"Just that she had a violent episode," Phil answered. "She's never done that before."

"Didn't you tell me once before that the facility she's in is one of the best for treating her form of dementia?"

"Yes, they are." *Thank goodness,* Phil thought.

"Which means you should stop worrying," Jamal interjected. "Your mother is in good hands, right?"

"Right," Phil said.

He reached over and held out his right hand. Phil hesitated for a moment before clasping it, and she was overwhelmed by the sense of relief that engulfed her. She held on to Jamal's hand like the lifeline it was, finding strength in his solid, comforting grip.

They made the drive in just under twenty minutes. Phil hopped out of the truck and half walked, half jogged to the entrance, leaving Jamal to follow. The receptionist's usually cheerful greeting had a layer of concern draped over it.

"Evelyn, where is she?" Phil asked the receptionist.

"She's in the infirmary," she said. "Have a seat and I'll call Dr. Beckman. He asked to be informed as soon as you arrived."

"Is she okay?" Phil asked.

"She's better." Evelyn nodded. "Just wait here."

Phil wrapped her arms around her waist. It took everything she had within her to keep from doubling over in fear. Her mother was all she had left, and on most days all Sabina Phillips had was her body. Her mind had long ago recessed to places that Phil rarely reached.

She could not stomach the thought of anything happening to her mother. She was shouldering so much already. Life could not be this cruel.

Phil's body hummed with awareness seconds before a set of warm arms surrounded her. She didn't even try to pull away. She just closed her eyes and soaked in the strength and security that enveloped her.

"Do you want to sit down?" Jamal whispered in her ear.

She shook her head, her throat too filled with emotion to utter a single word. They stood in the lobby for several minutes, the soft blue, green and light brown decor calming her, the refuge she found in Jamal's embrace bringing her an overwhelming peace. But when she spotted Dr. Timothy Beckman striding down the hallway, Phil tore away from Jamal's hold and headed for the facility's young director.

"Hello, Ms. Phillips," the man greeted, his slim, serene face looking less worried than she'd anticipated. Phil took that as a good sign.

"What happened with my mom?" she asked.

"She had a bit of an episode," Dr. Beckman said. "Can we talk about this in my office?"

"Can't I see her first?"

"Soon," he said. "The nurses are helping her change her clothing. They'll call my office as soon as they are done. Shall we go there to discuss what happened?"

Phil nodded. Dr. Beckman hesitated for a moment, looking beyond her shoulder.

"It's okay," she said. "He can come with me." She turned to Jamal. "That is, if you want to."

"Of course," he said, taking her hand and threading their fingers together. He gave her a firm squeeze, and Phil nearly crumbled to the ground in gratitude.

How could she have ever compared this man to Kevin, who would change the subject whenever Phil even mentioned her mother? Kevin didn't even know the name of this place, nor had he ever shown any interest in joining her when Phil had visited. Jamal Johnson was nothing like Kevin Winters.

Studying his profile, she realized he was unlike any of the men she'd dated in the past. Phil latched on to the comfort he offered, grateful she didn't have to go through this alone.

"Thank you," she whispered.

He glanced her way, and with a nod and an understanding smile, he simply said, "You're welcome."

Jamal held Phylicia's hand while the director of Mossy Oaks explained how her mother had violently pitched a glass vase against the wall in the residents' common area and disrupted a food cart laden with hot lunches. Dr. Beckman saw it as a sign that her mother's dementia was worsening.

"Patients become more aggressive as the disease progresses," he remarked.

"But this is so unlike her." Phylicia pressed a balled fist to her lips. "My mother has the gentlest soul of anyone I know."

"Remember we talked about this?" Dr. Beckman asked. "As the disease worsens, she will become less and less like her old self."

"I knew it was inevitable. I've read every article I could find on early-onset dementia." She shook her head. "It's just so hard to see it happening and know there's nothing anyone can do to stop it."

The slight tremble in her voice hit Jamal's chest like the sharp point of a javelin to his heart. He had to fight the urge to bring her hand to his lips and press a gentle kiss to her fingers. He settled for giving it another reassuring squeeze.

Dr. Beckman's desk phone rang. He picked it up, listened for a moment and said, "Thank you, Rebecca," before hanging up.

"Mrs. Phillips is back in her room. You still want to see her?"

"Of course," Phylicia said, springing up from the chair and leading the way out of the office. Jamal had to lengthen his stride just to keep up with her. As they approached the door to what he assumed was her mother's room, she glanced down at their joined hands then at him.

"Do you want to stay out here?" she asked.

"Only if you want me to," he answered.

She remained silent for several heartbeats before she said, "I'd like you to come in."

A strange feeling blossomed in Jamal's chest — a mixture of gladness, relief and a hint of fear that he couldn't fully describe. He swallowed, nodded and gripped her hand tighter as he followed her into the room.

Phylicia gave the door two sharp raps with her knuckle before easing it open.

"Mom?" she called with a soft voice.

They entered a comfortable-size room with a bed, television, two nightstands done in dark wood and a small seating area set up in front of a large window.

A woman, who looked so much like Phylicia that there could be no mistaking they were mother and daughter, sat in one of the high-backed chairs.

"Agatha?" the woman asked.

"Yes, Sabina, it's me," Phylicia said. She let go of his hand and made it to her mother's side in three strides.

Jamal held himself back, stopping just inside the door. The nurse who had been hovering next to Phylicia's mother walked toward where Jamal and Dr. Beckman stood.

"Is she okay?" Jamal asked.

The nurse nodded. "Especially now that Phylicia is here. Mrs. Phillips loves it when she visits, even though she mistakes her for her baby sister."

"Good work, Rebecca," Dr. Beckman said. He addressed Jamal. "I'll leave you all to visit. Use the call button next to the bed if you need anything."

Jamal nodded his thanks and shut the door behind the two as they exited, but he didn't move closer to Phylicia. He stood sentry at the door while she and her mother spoke in soft tones. Their closeness was evident in the way Phylicia gently caressed her mother's hand and the older woman smoothed the stray locks of hair away from Phylicia's face.

The ache that had pulsed in Jamal's chest grew tighter as he observed the mother and daughter. Unsurprisingly, his mind drifted to his own mother and how much he'd missed seeing her this past year.

The closeness he once shared with his mother and younger sister was, by far, the greatest casualty in this fallout between him and his dad. Not a single day went by that he didn't think about them.

Pride wouldn't allow him to admit to missing anything about his dad. As a father he had been sufficient but mostly missing in action, sacrificing time with his family in order to build his empire. As a boss he had been barely tolerable.

Jamal had always had a hard time separating the father from the CEO. His mother's unwavering support was given without question, but his father's approval had always had strings attached. It required blind allegiance to his ideals, and any opposition to his way of thinking was considered insurrection.

His life was just fine without Lawrence

Johnson, the head of Johnson Construction. Which meant he would have to do without Lawrence Johnson, the father, as well.

But did that mean he had to remain estranged from his mother and sister? Why should they continue to suffer from something that had nothing to do with them?

"Is this your new man, Agatha?" Jamal heard Phylicia's mother ask.

Phylicia's eyes flew to his. "Uh . . . yes, it is," she said as both she and her mother stood. Jamal saw the pleading in Phylicia's eyes as the women made their way over to where he stood.

The older version of Phylicia, who was as lithe and beautiful as her daughter, held her hand out.

"I'm Sabina, Agatha's older sister, but not by that many years."

Jamal captured her hand and placed a kiss on the back of her fingers. "I'm Jamal, and you are as beautiful and elegant as your younger sister."

She blushed and turned to Phylicia. "You've got yourself a charmer here, Agatha. I think he's a keeper."

"I think you may be right," Phylicia said, her huge brown eyes filled with gratitude and remorse and a myriad of other things that made the air in Jamal's lungs evaporate.

They all turned at a knock on the door. It was the nurse, Rebecca. "Sorry to disturb you all, but it's dinnertime," she said.

"No need to apologize," Phylicia said. "It's time we hit the road." She leaned over and gave her mother a kiss on the cheeck. "I'll be back to see you soon — tomorrow, if I can manage it."

"Oh, don't worry about coming here to see me, Agatha. You need to spend as much time with your young man as you can."

"I'll come with her," Jamal said, earning him a quick, surprised glance from Phylicia.

"Oh, yes, he's a good one," her mother said. She ushered them both out of the room. "Go on, now. And I'll see you two later."

They made their way out of Mossy Oaks in silence, neither saying a word until they were both seated in the truck. Phylicia reached over and put her hand on his forearm.

"Thank you," she said.

"It's no big deal," Jamal replied.

"It's a very big deal. I've been handling my mother's disease for three years by myself. I didn't realize how much I needed someone to lean on, especially after a day like today."

He reached over with his right hand and

moved a strand of hair from her face. "I'm happy I could be that person for you."

"So am I," she said.

The return trip to Gauthier was made with very little communication between them, just the occasional comment about houses they passed or other drivers on the road. There was so much more he wanted to say, but every time he started to speak about what happened back at Mossy Oaks, Jamal stopped himself. He could sense that Phylicia needed space.

He pulled into her driveway and parked. The logical thing would have been to have her drop him off at Belle Maison, where he'd left his truck, but he didn't think Phylicia should be driving.

"I can call Corey, have him pick me up," Jamal suggested.

She looked down at her lap, then over at him. "Would you mind coming in?" she asked in a soft voice. "Just for a few minutes."

The relief that flooded him was enough to drown a small village. "Absolutely," Jamal said.

He got out of the truck and followed her into the house. The silence continued as Phylicia flipped on the lights and walked to the kitchen. Jamal wasn't sure what he should say. He decided to come right out with the question that had been weighing on his mind.

"How long has your mother been sick?" he asked.

Phylicia opened the refrigerator and pulled out two cans of Coca-Cola. She handed him one and popped hers open, taking a healthy sip before leaning back against the counter and crossing her arms over her chest.

"She started showing signs about five years ago. She would go to the grocery store and forget why she went there. Or she would ask the same questions several times a day, sometimes only a few minutes after she'd asked it.

"In the beginning it wasn't anything that would raise a red flag, but it soon became apparent that something wasn't right. I put her in Mossy Oaks three years ago, just a few months after my dad died."

She shook her head, staring at the floor. "It killed me to do that. I felt like such a failure. After everything she and my dad had done for me, I pay her back by putting her in a home."

"Not just any home," he said. "You put her in the care of people who know how to deal with her illness. You did the responsible thing."

"It didn't feel like it at the time. It felt as if I was shirking my responsibility." Phylicia finally looked up at him again, and the sheen of tears glistening in her eyes tore at Jamal's heart.

"I just couldn't handle her on my own." Her voice trembled. She shook her head, wrapping her arms around her middle. "I would come home and find dinner burned beyond recognition, or I'd find her wandering the neighborhood. Once, she took a trowel and uprooted all the flowers in Mrs. Jacobs's landscaping." She sniffed and wiped her nose with the back of her hand. "I was afraid she would burn the house down, or wander somewhere and get hurt."

"Taking care of an elderly parent is a tough job," he said.

"Did that woman look elderly to you?" Phylicia practically shouted. "I'm sorry," she said. "It's just so unfair. She's only sixty-two years old. She's in tip-top shape, but her mind is just completely gone."

Jamal had tried to maintain his distance, give her the space she needed. But as soon as he saw the tears start to roll down her cheeks, he pushed away from the kitchen island and was at her side. Relief sank into his bones when she allowed him to wrap his arms around her.

She buried her face against his chest, her shoulders shaking with her silent sobs.

"It's as if I've lost both of them," she murmured.

"I'm so sorry," Jamal whispered against her hair. He smoothed his hands up and down her back, providing comfort the only way he could. "You and your mother were close. I could tell just by looking at the two of you today."

"When I was in grade school, she would just show up out of the blue with a pan of brownies for the entire class. It made me very popular," Phylicia said with a soft chuckle. It was the first hint of levity Jamal had heard in her voice in weeks. He loved hearing her laugh.

"I miss having my parents in my life," she continued. "We were such a close family. Mom considered herself the disciplinarian of the family, because she said I had my dad wrapped around my little finger from the minute I was born."

"Did you?" he asked.

"Oh, yeah. When it came to my dad, I could get away with just about anything." She sniffed and wiped the cheek that wasn't nestled against his chest. "I swear I would give anything to take back that last conversation we had. Not a day goes by that I don't regret it."

Jamal pulled her slightly away so he could look her in the eyes. "You know he probably forgave you the minute you walked away from him, right?"

"I know he did," she said. "That's just the type of person he was. But it doesn't change how I feel. I hurt him, Jamal. And it just kills me that the last words we shared were filled with so much anger." She looked up at him, her eyes pleading and filled with self-reproach. "Don't make the same mistake I made. I know you and your dad don't see eye to eye, but living with this kind of regret is soul sucking. You need to talk to him. Just get it all out in the open and forgive each other. It's not worth this kind of pain."

Jamal's back stiffened, but he neither acquiesced nor verbally dismissed her plea. Instead, he gently lowered her head back onto his chest and trailed his hand along her hair.

Jamal stood in the middle of her kitchen for a long, unhurried stretch of time, holding her, infusing strength, providing solace. After a while, Phylicia disengaged from his embrace. She swiped at her tear-streaked cheeks and grabbed a paper towel, using it to wipe her face.

"I'm sorry about that," she said, pointing to the spots of moisture she'd left on his shirt.

"No need to apologize," he said.

She looked so exposed, so vulnerable, Jamal wanted nothing more than to pull her into his arms again. God, he wanted to hold her. His body burned with the remembered feel of her against him.

Less than two feet separated them as they faced each other, and the charged air circulating in that space was saturated with a bevy of unspoken emotions. But the one that surpassed everything else was desire.

He felt like a complete dog, wanting her the way he did after everything she'd been through today. But he couldn't help it. His body yearned for hers, for the comfortable bed just down the hallway, for the pleasure they could both give each other if only they could erase the tension from the past few weeks.

God, how he wished they could go back to the afternoon when they'd explored each other's bodies underneath that oak tree. What he wouldn't give to eradicate what had happened when they'd returned to the Victorian to discover her mother's painting room destroyed.

If only he could erase it. It would make

everything in his world right again.

Her next words had the effect of an anvil crushing his chest.

"You should probably go," she said in a quiet, but firm voice. "Thank you again for coming with me today."

"Phylicia —"

She held up a hand. "Don't, Jamal. It's just not a good idea."

"Yes, it is," he challenged. He knew he wasn't being fair, was probably crossing a line that he shouldn't cross, but dammit, he missed her.

"You can't tell me you haven't been miserable these past few weeks, Phylicia. I dread even going to the house in the morning, because it's so damn hard to work near you and not touch you. To have you ignore me. Do you know how much that kills me?"

She pulled her trembling bottom lip between her teeth. "You're going to hurt me," she said in a small voice. "You may not even realize it, but you will. It always happens."

He captured her hands and brought them to his lips. "Not this time," Jamal said. "I promise you, Phylicia. I will never, ever do anything to hurt you."

She pulled in a deep breath and blew it out in a rush. "This is such a mistake."

"Stop saying that," Jamal said. He leaned forward, pressing his forehead to hers as he looked into her eyes. "Nothing about us being together could ever be a mistake, Phylicia. The two of us together . . . it just makes sense."

Jamal could tell when she relented. The rigidity in her limbs eased, and she melted against him. He captured her chin and tipped her face up, sealing his mouth to hers as he ran his other hand down her spine, to her soft, perfectly shaped rear end. He pulled her more firmly against him, nestling his hardening body against her soft warmth.

"Don't make me regret this," she pleaded.

"Never," Jamal whispered against her lips.

Without another word, Phylicia took him by the hand and led him to her bedroom.

CHAPTER 12

Phil awoke the next morning with a start, springing up from the pillow and glancing around the room.

"What's the matter?" came Jamal's sleep-roughened voice.

Her entire body relaxed with languid relief. He was still here.

"Nothing." She eased back onto the pillows, and Jamal stretched an arm around her, pulling her against his side. He pressed a kiss to her bare shoulder.

"We should probably get up," he said.

"Probably," Phil replied.

"I don't really want to," he admitted.

A smile lifted the corner of her mouth. "Neither do I."

She stretched, lining her body up against his corded muscles. A shiver of desire ran through her as she felt his erection coming to life against her thigh.

"We definitely don't have time for *that*."

She laughed.

"I can be really quick when I have to," he murmured against her shoulder.

"But then you'll just want to do it again," Phil said, disengaging from his hold and scooting off the bed.

"God, you're sexy," Jamal said, his eyes heating her skin as they ran up and down her naked body.

"Stop looking at me like that."

"Like what?"

"Like I'm breakfast."

He crooked a finger, but by a force of will she didn't know she possessed, Phil stopped herself from diving back under the covers.

"I'm going to shower," she said. "And, no, you can't join me," she added. "The new shutters are being delivered to Belle Maison this morning. I want to inspect them before signing for the delivery."

"Dammit. I forgot all about that." Jamal pushed himself up from the bed. "We need to swing by my place so I can change."

Phil just stared at the absolute perfection of his well-honed muscles and flawless physique.

"If you don't want me in the shower with you, you'd better stop looking at me like that," he warned.

The humorous, cocky gleam in his eyes

was just what she needed to douse her body's amorous cravings. He was just a little too sure of himself.

"I'll be ready in ten minutes," she said. "And I'd appreciate a cup of coffee waiting for me."

She closed the door behind her and heard, "God, I love a bossy woman," come from the other side.

A half hour later they were pulling up to Jamal's home. Once inside he gave her a swift kiss and said, "I won't be too long. Just a quick shower and a change of clothes. Make yourself at home."

She wiggled her empty travel mug. "Is there a coffeemaker?"

"More coffee?"

"Well, someone kept me up way too late last night," she returned.

He shot her a wicked grin and pointed her in the direction of the coffeemaker, and Phil set about making another pot. She walked over to the refrigerator in search of cream and noticed the wedding announcement and RSVP for Jamal's sister's wedding stuck to the stainless steel refrigerator with a magnet. She pulled it off the refrigerator and read over the embossed writing.

When Jamal walked into the kitchen, Phil pointed to the response card. "You haven't sent this off yet?" she asked.

His shoulders visibly sank. "Don't bring that up. Please."

"Jamal, think of how much it would hurt your sister if you missed her wedding."

His face turned so grim he hardly resembled the same man she'd spent the night with.

"Not just Lauryn. My mom, too," he said. He looked over at her. "There was a message from her on my voice mail, asking again if I would make the wedding."

"You have to go, Jamal. They're your family. Be grateful you still have them."

He stared at her for several moments, before saying, "Come with me."

Phil's spine stiffened. "What?"

"Come with me to Arizona."

She shook her head and took a step back. "That's crossing a line between client and employee that definitely should not be crossed."

"We're more than just client and employee, Phylicia."

She shook her head. "Not until I finish the job on Belle Maison," she said.

Jamal rolled his eyes. "Fine, then consider it a business trip." He paused for a beat, his eyes widening with interest. "That's actually not a bad idea," he continued. "There are several bed-and-breakfasts out there that I'd like to see. We can leave a couple of days early and check out a few of them. I can interview the owners, see how they operate."

"I can't leave my mom," Phil said, even as the thought of spending a few days touring parts of Arizona with Jamal sent tremors of delight up her spine.

"It would only be for a couple of days. If something happens while we're away, I can get you back here in a matter of hours. Johnson Construction has two private jets. I'd suck it up and ask for permission to use one of them if necessary."

He closed the distance between them and wrapped his arms around her waist, resting his hands at the small of her back.

"Come with me," he urged. "Arizona is beautiful this time of the year. I want to show you my home state. And," he continued, "if I'm going to occupy the same space as my dad, I could use the support."

Phil couldn't believe she was actually contemplating this. Not only was she contemplating it, she was going to say yes.

What happened to learning from her mistakes? This had potential disaster written all over it. She would be out of her element and completely at Jamal's mercy, because God knows she couldn't afford to fly herself back home if she had to quickly get back to Gauthier.

Yet, despite the objections bouncing back and forth in her mind, Phil heard herself say, "Okay, I'll join you."

"This house looks amazing!" Mya shouted from the front lawn.

Jamal waved at her from his perch on the ladder, earning a stern frown from Phylicia. He tightened the final screw in the antique hanging light fixture he and Phylicia had found at a salvage yard in Mississippi last weekend, then he made his way down the ladder.

Jamal laughed as Mya waddled up the porch steps. He pulled her in for a quick kiss on the cheek and motioned to her stomach. "How much longer until you let this baby out?"

"Five weeks, and not a moment later," she said. "If she's not ready to come out, I'm going in after her." She gestured to the freshly painted porch. "Everything looks wonderful."

"Thanks," both he and Phylicia said at the same time. They looked at each other and chuckled.

"The contractors did a really good job. I

was afraid the work would be sloppy," Phylicia said.

"That's because you think anybody's work but your own is sloppy," Mya teased.

"Because it usually is," she quipped.

"There's not much left to do," Jamal added. "A few touch-ups here and there, but that's it. The furniture will be delivered the day after we get back from Arizona."

"Ah, yes," Mya said, dragging out the word. "Arizona. You two leave in the morning, right?"

Phylicia rolled her eyes. "Just say 'I told you so' and get it over with."

"I wasn't going to say anything," Mya returned.

Jamal's mouth twitched in amusement as he watched the two of them go at it. His cell phone rang, so he stepped away, leaving them to their debate.

"Hello?" he answered.

"Hello, Mr. Johnson." Jamal recognized his Realtor's voice. "There's been an offer on the Saint Charles Avenue property. Have you decided whether or not you want it?"

"I . . ." he started, but his voice fell silent.

He didn't know what the hell he wanted.

On one hand, it would be the ultimate payback to go to Arizona with the bill of sale to the building of his very own architectural firm in his hands . . . and shove it down his old man's throat.

But if he bought that building, Jamal knew there would be no more excuses.

And if this venture didn't work out, *he* would be the one who would have to eat his own words. His hand balled into a fist. He could just envision his father's mocking, triumphant face.

"Mr. Johnson?" his Realtor prompted.

"I . . . uh . . . I need just a few more days," he said. "I'm going out of town for the weekend, but I'll have an answer by Monday."

"Are you sure, Mr. Johnson? You're taking a chance at losing this property. Are you sure you're willing to risk that?"

Not only was he willing to risk it, Jamal *hoped* something like that would happen. If another buyer scooped up the house, he'd have to go back to square one and start the long process of searching for another suitable location. He would be off the hook . . . at least for a few more months.

Disgust churned in his gut, even as relief sank into his bones. Could he really be this much of a damn coward?

"Just . . ." Jamal cleared his throat. "Just give me the weekend. I'll have an answer for you by Monday."

He ended the call and shoved the phone back in his pocket with more force than necessary. He took a moment to shake off the self-loathing eating away at him before walking over to the Victorian's east lawn, where Phylicia was showing Mya the new gazebo that had been constructed this week.

"Jamal is having custom-made cushions installed to match the fabric on the other outdoor furniture," she was saying. She looked over at him and frowned. "Is everything okay?"

"I'm fine," Jamal lied.

"Are you sure?" She cocked her head at an angle. "You look . . . I don't know . . . off."

"I'm fine," he repeated, dismissing her concern with a nonchalant wave. He turned to Mya and draped an arm across her shoulders. "Think you can handle a tour of the inside?"

"Absolutely," Mya said, beaming.

His diversion technique sufficiently put an end to Phylicia's questioning, but it tripled his outright disgust with himself. Not only was he a coward, but a liar, too.

Because one thing was for certain. He definitely was *not* fine.

CHAPTER 13

Anxiety gripped Jamal's stomach as soon as the wheels of the plane touched ground at Phoenix's Sky Harbor International Airport. The sickening feeling had been building in his gut throughout the duration of the flight, and right now, he wanted nothing more than to book a return flight to New Orleans. Leaving now.

"You look about as comfortable as a catfish in a seafood restaurant," Phylicia said.

"Try a catfish next to a fry pan filled with hot oil," he said.

She reached over and took his hand. "It'll be okay. You're going to be relieved once you and your father have aired out your differences."

"I don't plan to air out anything with him," Jamal said. "I'm here for my sister and my mother. If I could, I would go this entire trip without even seeing my father."

"Jamal, you cannot come all this way and

230

not speak to him."

"Watch me," he said.

"But —"

"Phylicia, let it go. Please," he pleaded in a softer tone. "I don't want to ruin our time together arguing over this. Let me handle this thing with my father my way, okay?"

She started to speak, but then relented. Holding her palms up, she said, "Fine. Miss this golden opportunity to set things right if you want to." She shot him a pointed look. "Just remember that you may not get another."

"I'll take my chances." He hoisted her carry-on bag over his shoulder and they deplaned. After retrieving the rest of the luggage from baggage claim, they walked over to the rental car kiosk and were shuttled to their waiting car.

Jamal headed north on Interstate 17, soaking in the familiar surroundings. Phylicia twisted around in her seat to observe all the sights.

"The most I've ever seen of Phoenix is the view from the airport. Whenever I fly to the West Coast, the layover is either here or Las Vegas," she explained.

"Phoenix is a great city."

"Do you miss it?"

He shrugged. "Haven't been gone long

enough to miss it yet," he said. The lie tasted bitter on his tongue. He'd missed his hometown more than he ever thought he would. He missed the fresh air and the gorgeous sunsets. He missed checking out a Diamondbacks game on a weekday afternoon.

He missed his family.

An ache settled in his chest at the thought of his family. Before leaving Arizona, the longest he'd ever gone without seeing his mother was a week — even when he was in college. Not seeing both his mother and Lauryn had been, by far, the biggest adjustment to his new life.

And yet, he wasn't ready to face them. Not yet. Because seeing his mother and sister meant he'd have to endure his father's company. He wanted to enjoy being back home for a few days before having to brave that reunion.

Jamal continued driving north on I-17. After about a half hour, when Phoenix proper was well behind them, Phylicia twisted in her seat and looked at him.

"Just how far does your family live from the city?"

"We're not going to my family's house," Jamal said. "Remember, the first part of this trip is for research. I booked us a room at a bed-and-breakfast in Sedona. It is one of the most beautiful areas in all of Arizona."

"How far is Sedona?"

"About another hour and a half," he said.

She shot him an incredulous frown. "So we're staying two hours away from where the wedding will take place?"

"It's worth the drive," Jamal said. "I promise."

"But —"

He leaned over and kissed the question right out of her mouth. He knew she'd bring up the issue between him and his dad, and Jamal wasn't up to dealing with it. He'd orchestrated a relaxing, romantic getaway, and he wasn't about to let Phylicia spoil it with her peacemaking attempts. He would be the one to decide whether or not he made peace with his father.

Phylicia spent the remainder of the drive into Verde Valley peppering him with questions about each and every mountain and stretch of desert they passed. As they approached the idyllic mountain ranges of the northeast region, Jamal was pretty sure she would stroke out from her excitement.

"This is absolutely gorgeous," she gasped.

"They call this Red Rock Country," Jamal explained. "I'm going to take you on a tour of it tomorrow and show you two of the most famous formations, Cathedral Rock and Thunder Mountain. I can promise you've never seen anything more beautiful."

The car's navigation system indicated that they should exit the highway, and a few minutes later, the sign for the Creekside Bed-and-Breakfast came into view. They were greeted by the husband and wife who owned and operated the B&B. After checking in, they were treated to a tour of the public areas.

"As you can see, the house is all Arizona on the outside, but inside we have traditional Victorian furnishings and decor."

"That's the reason I picked this B&B," Jamal said. "We're in the process of renovating an 1870s Victorian in Louisiana. I'm hoping to pick your brains a bit on what has worked and what hasn't with Creekside."

"Congratulations," the woman said. "You will love it." She wagged a finger in their direction. "And don't let anyone tell you that you shouldn't work together as husband and wife. We've done it for several years, and it has only added to our marriage."

Jamal glanced at Phylicia to see if she would correct the woman's erroneous assumption. His chest tightened with unbearable hope when she didn't. The thought of being mistaken for Phylicia's husband didn't scare him nearly as much as he thought it would. In fact, the thought of the two of them operating Belle Maison together sent a deliciously intoxicating spike of pleasure coursing through his bloodstream.

"The two of you will be lodging in the Sovereign Suite, one of our most ornate . . . and romantic," the B&B owner tacked on.

Standing along the bank of gurgling Oak Creek that ran right through the property, Jamal couldn't help but grin at Phylicia's animated rambling.

"I honestly do not believe I have seen anything this beautiful in my entire life. Look at it," she said. "And listen. How soothing is that? It sounds like one of those nature CDs." She turned to him. "Why didn't you tell me to bring my paints? How peaceful would it be to stand here with my easel?"

The water rushing over and around the smooth rocks was calming, but the mention of painting supplies reminded Jamal of the last time she'd painted outside, surrounded by nature. Making love to her there would be a lifelong memory. He was suddenly anxious to get her inside the house.

"Why don't we check out the room?" he asked.

Phylicia frowned, but when Jamal lifted his brows in a knowing look, a delicate pink hue blossomed high on her cheeks. She knew exactly what he was suggesting.

The innkeeper informed them of dinnertime, but Jamal wasn't thinking about food. The only thing he needed right now was Phylicia, good and naked.

When they finally arrived in their room, he didn't register anything about their surroundings except for the bed. Tumbling onto the mass of frilly bedding, he stripped Phylicia out of her clothes and spent the next half hour exploring the terrains of her body. He licked up and down the peaks of her firm breasts and trailed kisses along the smooth hollow of her gently concave stomach. He gripped her faintly rounded hips and used his tongue to explore the delicious world between her legs.

When they were done, they both collapsed onto the bed and stared up at the ceiling, puffing out exhausted and contented breaths.

"I would love to see what the rest of the room looks like," Phylicia said. "But I'm too tired to move."

"We're here for two nights," Jamal said. "There's time to see the room."

She scooted closer to him and snuggled

with her back against his chest, pulling his arm across her torso. Jamal snaked a hand up to cup her breast, relishing in the softness.

"I can spend the next two days and nights right here, just like this," Phylicia said.

"You'd get no complaints from me," he told her. "We don't have to go anywhere. We can see the wineries another time."

She glanced over her bare shoulder. "Wineries?"

He nodded. "There are several in the area. I scheduled a few tastings. I'm hoping I can set up a deal with one of them to provide wines for the B&B. But I can do that another time."

"No, you won't," she told him. "I've never been to a winery before." She twisted until she faced him, resting her chin in her upturned palm, her eyes bright with excitement. "I wonder if I can stomp the grapes like in that episode of *I Love Lucy*. I've always wanted to do that."

"Why? It looks messy as hell."

"True." She laughed. "But you have to admit it looks fun."

"Actually," Jamal said, capturing her waist and pulling her on top of him, "I can think of something that's *way* more fun than stomping grapes."

■ ■ ■ ■

"This. Is. *Gorgeous!*"

Jamal grinned at Phylicia's enthusiasm, feeding off the excitement that shone through her bright eyes. They stood amidst rows of waist-high vines that stretched as far as the eye could see, the warm Arizona sun beating down on them.

"This soil is ideal for producing a sweet, fragrant harvest," their personal tour guide explained. "This region's wines are known for their distinct flavor."

They forayed deeper into the vineyard and were treated to plump, juicy grapes right off the vine. When the tour was done, they were led past the small restaurant and into a private tasting room where several bottles were set up.

Once they were done with their tasting, Jamal talked business with the vineyard's owner, but he kept an eye on Phylicia as she explored the beautiful woodworking of the intricately carved wine racks.

"Nice work," Jamal said, coming up behind her.

She ran her hand along the wood. "It is. This took a lot of time." She looked back at him over her shoulder. "I can make you one like this, you know. Something on a smaller scale to hold your wines at Belle Maison."

"I may have to take you up on that," he said. He leaned over and whispered in her ear, "But, right now, I have a surprise for you."

There was a quizzical lift to her brow.

"It's time to stomp some grapes," he said.

She gasped. "Are you kidding me?" She pointed toward the door where their tour guide had just left. "But she said new regulations prevent the vineyard from using that method."

Jamal shrugged. "I pulled a few strings."

The look she graced him with was akin to a kid getting the toy she'd been hoping for on her birthday, and Jamal couldn't help the way his chest puffed out a bit. He could get used to being the hero.

They were brought into a room filled with huge barrels lining the walls. On an elevated platform stood a wooden tub. Jamal followed Phylicia up the stairs, and after washing her feet with the supplies that were provided, helped her into the tub filled with freshly picked grapes.

"Oh, my goodness," she said. "This feels so weird."

"Looks pretty sexy to me," Jamal said, staring at the smooth thighs that peeked from under the dress she held in her hands.

"Aren't you joining me?" she asked.

"Nah, I'd rather watch."

She pulled her bottom lip between her teeth as she gingerly took her first couple of steps. "This is *so* weird," she said again. "But, um, kind of fun."

Jamal looked on as her attack on the grapes became more aggressive. The only other time he'd seen Phylicia this uninhibited was when she was painting, and never had he seen her so playful. He loved the way it looked on her. She had so many burdens weighing her down — guilt over her father, worry about her mother's health, stress from that jerk of an ex who'd left her in near financial ruin. The chance to put a smile on her face was worth the extravagant price he'd paid for this little excursion.

"You don't know what you're missing." Phylicia grinned.

"I'll take your word for it," Jamal returned as he studied the unbelievably sexy way the delicate muscles in her lean legs flexed with her movements. The hem of her dress brushed her thighs, driving him out of his mind.

After she'd stomped around for nearly twenty minutes, he was finally able to coax her out of the tub. They were shown to a washroom where Phylicia was able to clean her legs and feet. Even *that* was sexy.

His phone vibrated and Jamal checked the screen. It was the event planner he'd hired, letting him know that everything was set for the other bit of extravagance he had planned.

"Are you ready?" he asked her.

"Are we going to another winery?"

"No, I think I'm going to go with this one as my Arizona supplier. When we get back to Louisiana I'll visit a few and get another local supplier. But we need to get on the road." He gestured with his head.

"Where're we going now?"

"I promised to show you my home state's magnificent scenery, remember?" He captured her hand and placed a delicate kiss on the back of her fingers. "We still have a lot to explore."

Jamal purchased a couple of bottles of wine from the winery before heading for Route 179 to Cathedral Rock. A short time later, he pulled the rental car into the driveway of the Crescent Moon Ranch.

"Is that it?" Phylicia asked, pointing to the majestic red rock with its two peaks.

"Yep," Jamal said as he grabbed a bottle of wine. "Let's walk. There's an even better view on the other side of the cabin. It's the best place to watch the sunset."

They rounded the corner and Phylicia's loud gasp echoed around them. Dozens of lit candles surrounded a hand-stitched blanket with a traditional Native American design. A picnic basket, filled with bread, fruit and several artisan cheeses delivered from a dairy farm in Tempe, sat just to the right of it.

She whirled around, her eyes wide with surprise. "How did you do this?"

"I told you I would show you the best that Arizona has to offer. Sit." He gestured to the blanket with his head.

After settling next to her on the colorful blanket, Jamal filled the two wine glasses Phylicia held, then opened his legs so she could scoot between them. He wrapped an arm around her middle and nestled his lips against her neck.

"Thank you for coming here with me," he said. "You've made an unbearable trip better than I ever thought possible. Instead of being miserable, I'm actually enjoying myself."

"You're welcome," she said. After a pregnant pause, she quietly asked, "Jamal, what was the argument with your dad about?"

He shook his head, rubbing his chin against her collarbone. "I don't want to talk about it," he murmured.

"No," she said with enough force to make him rear back a bit. She twisted around and faced him with a look that said she wasn't backing down. "You don't get to shrug this question off anymore. I came all this way to be here for you when you face your dad. The least you can do is tell me what caused the disagreement in the first place. What did he do that was so horrible?"

"It wasn't just one thing," Jamal answered. He blew out a frustrated breath, casting his gaze on the red rock formation in the distance. "My father doesn't respect me. He never has."

"What makes you think that?"

"Because he practically said it to my face." Jamal drained the remainder of his wine and set the glass down, silently applauding himself for not grabbing the bottle and drinking straight from it. Talking about this would be so much easier after an entire bottle of wine. Or four.

"One morning, my dad came into my office and told me to pack up because I was moving to the twenty-eighth floor, into one of the executive suites. I told him I was fine with my windowless office on the sixth floor, with the rest of the architects at Johnson Construction. But he'd never intended for his only son to remain a lowly architect.

"It's time for you to step up to the plate and take a swing at being the boss,' " Jamal mimicked in his father's voice. "He's the king of baseball analogies," he said with a derisive snort.

"You must have known he had this in mind. How long had he been grooming you to move up into a leadership role at the company?"

"Since birth," Jamal answered. "But I never wanted it. Never. It's the creation process that I love. I love working with my hands, even when it's only my hands touching the keyboard and computer mouse. I've never wanted to be anyone's boss."

"But you will be when you open your firm and hire people."

"Yeah, but it won't be the same," he said. "For one thing, my firm will be a one-man show for at least the first year. I'll expand in the future, but I don't want it to grow into what Johnson Construction has become." He shook his head. "I can remember a time when my dad knew the name of every person who worked for him. Now, there are twenty thousand employees.

"I'm going to make sure that my firm remains small, and more of a partnership than one man at the top dictating what others do. I'm going to be open-minded when it comes to new ideas. The complete opposite of my father."

"Ah, let me guess," Phil said. "He isn't on board with the eco-friendly stuff?"

"Somebody hand the lady a prize," Jamal said, his mouth twisting with a cynical grin. "I'd been waiting for the perfect opportunity to share some of my ideas for incorporating green technology into Johnson Construction's designs. But that morning was definitely *not* the time to do it. Things went downhill from there. I told him if he wasn't ready to step into the twenty-first century, I would just open my own firm."

Phylicia's eyes widened. "What did he say to that?"

"That I didn't have what it takes to make it on my own. That I'd come crawling back to Johnson Construction with my hands stretched out."

"He did not!" Phylicia gasped, her vehemence on his behalf providing a small measure of comfort.

"It shouldn't have hurt me as much as it did. It wasn't the first time he'd shot down my ideas. I was used to it." A familiar pang of disappointment tightened Jamal's chest. "I'd spent my entire life trying to live up to his expectations, and . . . I don't know . . . I just . . . I was just over it. At that point, I knew I'd never earn that man's respect.

"It was time for me to go," Jamal said. "I was tired of having my life dictated by other people."

Phylicia caressed his cheek, a sympathetic frown marring her brow. "I'm sorry," she said. She gazed up at him for several hauntingly quiet moments before she spoke again in a soft voice. "Jamal, don't take this the wrong way, but why haven't you opened your firm?"

Her question struck a chord of panic in his chest, but he shrugged it off. "I want to take my time and make sure I do it right."

"But you're not making any progress on it," she said. "You've spent over a year working first on the Georgian, and now Belle Maison. You haven't even decided on a location for your firm."

"I'm not in any big rush, Phylicia."

"Because there's no reason for you to rush. You have enough money to live on for the rest of your life. You can put off opening this firm forever." She tilted her head to the side, those brown eyes boring into his. "If this is something you truly want, why haven't you made more of an effort to see it through, Jamal?"

Jamal tried to keep his expression light,

but unease tightened his jaw. "What's with the third degree?" he asked with an uncomfortable laugh.

"You're afraid," she said.

Her simple, softly spoken words hit a raw nerve.

"You don't know what you're talking about."

"I know exactly what I'm talking about," she said. "I know what it's like to be afraid to fail, Jamal. When that house-flipping venture went bad, I tried to put all of the blame on Kevin, but I was just as culpable. I wanted to prove to myself that I was right in wanting to expand my father's business."

"Our situations are completely different."

"No, they're not." She placed her soft palm against his cheek, her eyes brimming with understanding. "You have something to prove, just as I did. And just like me, you're afraid that if you fail, you'll prove your father right. That's why you took so long to remodel your house, and why you bought Belle Maison. You're finding projects to occupy your time so that you don't have to go after your dream."

He huffed out a grunt. "I thought your degree was in finance, not psychology," he said, reaching for the wine. He busied himself with refilling his glass so he wouldn't

247

have to face the truth that pummeled him with every word Phylicia uttered.

She took the bottle from his hands and set it next to them.

"It doesn't take a psychology degree to see what's going on here," she said. "Don't let fear stop you. And don't let revenge or some misguided desire to prove your dad wrong be your sole focus. This is *your* dream. Do it for *you.*

"And, Jamal?" She captured his chin between her fingers and tilted his head up. "You need to settle things with your dad. Don't let it eat away at your family anymore," she pleaded. "It's not worth it. Trust me on this."

"Phylicia, let me handle this in my own time."

"But —"

Jamal leaned forward and captured her lips, halting further comment. He had not gone to all this trouble setting up this romantic night just to ruin it with talk of his father.

"Enough free advice for the night," he whispered against her lips. "We've got other ways to occupy our time."

CHAPTER 14

A toxic mixture of anxiety, fear and a healthy dose of disgust roiled through Jamal's gut as they made their way to the Aztec Ballroom of the Biltmore Hotel, where his sister's wedding and reception were being held. With each step he took, Jamal had to talk himself out of turning around and driving back to Sedona.

He knew it was out of the question. He'd come here for Lauryn. He was not going to ruin her big day. He and Lawrence Johnson would just have to suck it up and tolerate each other's presence.

Jamal glanced over at Phylicia, who had an excellent chance of outshining the bride. She was stunning in the form-fitting strapless gray dress. Her subtle makeup transformed her face into a thing of breath-stealing beauty. Jamal could spend hours staring at her.

"Stop staring at me like that," she said in

a hushed voice.

"I can't help it," Jamal said. "You're just so damn good to stare at."

The blush that blossomed on her cheeks made looking at her even more enjoyable. He loved making her blush. He'd figured out so many ways to do it over the past few months.

"Are you ready for this?" Phylicia asked.

Her inquiry doused his heated thoughts. Sucking in a heavy breath, Jamal answered, "As ready as I'll ever be."

As soon as they entered the elegant ballroom, Jamal heard a sharp gasp. He turned and, a second later, was enveloped in a set of warm, familiar arms.

"Oh, Jamal," his mother cried. She grabbed his face and kissed both of his cheeks.

"Don't cry. You'll ruin your makeup," he teased. It was either make jokes or bawl along with her. God, how he'd missed this woman. "It's great to see you, Mom."

She cradled his cheek in her palm. "Oh, you, too, darling. I've missed you so much. It isn't the same with you being away."

Jamal took her hand and kissed the back of her fingers. He turned to Phylicia, who'd stood a few feet back. The emotion on her face nearly did Jamal in. He realized that she could no longer have moments like this with her mother.

In that instant, the anxiety over returning to Arizona withered and died. He was blessed with a healthy, vibrant mother who meant the world to him, and he'd purposely stayed away because of his father? How selfish — *how foolish* — could he be? He was never staying away this long again.

Jamal turned to Phylicia. "Mother, this is my date, Phylicia Phillips. Phylicia, my mother, Katherine Johnson."

"It's so nice to meet you," Phylicia said, taking her hand. "And this place is absolutely beautiful."

"So are you," his mother returned, her eyes widening with unconcealed curiosity. "How did you two meet?"

"You remember Corey Anderson, my old roommate at Arizona State?" Jamal asked. "He and Phylicia went to high school together. She's a restoration specialist in Louisiana. She's helping me to restore the home that I'm turning into a bed-and-breakfast."

"Oh, what fascinating work. You and Jamal must have so much in common. I'm guessing you've been spending a lot of time together?" Her voice was so hopeful, Jamal had to bite back a laugh.

"Um . . . yes, we have," Phylicia said, her eyes darting his way, sparkling with amusement. "Your son has very unique ideas when it comes to design."

"He's a brilliant architect, and a great provider. He can play the saxophone, too. And I just know he's going to be a wonderful father someday. He just needs to find the right woman."

Oh, great. *Way to be subtle, Mom.* He wouldn't be surprised if she pulled out a résumé listing his husbandly qualities.

Glancing around the room, Jamal spotted his father heading toward them.

His jaw stiffened. "I'm going to find Lauryn and say hello before the ceremony begins," he said. "Phylicia, I'll only be a few minutes."

Covering his forearm with her gloved hand, his mother looked at him with mournful eyes. "Jamal, talk to him," she said.

The pleading in her voice clawed at his soul, but as Jamal took in the arrogant, haughty look on his father's face, he knew that any confrontation between them right now would make his sister's wedding a spectacle instead of the magical day she deserved. He kissed his mother's cheek and turned, heading for the opposite side of the vast ballroom.

By the time he found the suite where his sister and her bridesmaids were getting dressed, Jamal had only a few moments to talk to her. After being away for over a year, it wasn't nearly long enough.

By the time he returned to Phylicia, the ceremony was beginning.

As the night wore on, it became evident that he and his father were on the same page when it came to getting through the evening. They put equal amounts of effort into avoiding each other. Even during the family photos, when they stood mere feet from one another, not a single word was spoken between them.

That was just fine with him, Jamal thought. Until he noticed the sadness in his mother's eyes. The sorrow evident on her face hit him square in the chest.

"Are you okay?" Phylicia asked as he rejoined her at their table.

Jamal reached for her hand and brought it to his lips. "I'm good," he said. "Especially with you here with me."

The lead singer of the live band that had covered songs from the nineties announced that it was time for the traditional bride and groom dance, but instead of going to the center of the ballroom, his sister headed for the stage and gestured for the microphone.

"Hello again, everyone," Lauryn started, that smile she'd been wearing all night as bright as ever. "I hope you all are enjoying yourselves and adding up a huge tab at the bar, since my dad is paying for it all." Laughter flittered around the room. "Michael and I had picked out a song for this dance, but at the time I didn't know if my big brother, Jamal, would be here." She looked directly at him, her brown eyes, so much like his, softening. "Since he is, I would be so honored if our wedding song came from his saxophone. Jamal, will you play for us?"

Without hesitation, Jamal set his drink on the table and made his way to the stage.

"You know that I usually don't play another person's sax," he told his sister. "But for you, I'll make an exception."

Lauryn's face beamed. She stood on her tiptoes and kissed his cheek. "Thank you, big brother. You shouldn't even have to ask which song," she said.

Jamal glanced over at the sheet music on the stand and let out a sharp crack of laughter. "I should have guessed," he said.

He positioned his fingers on the keys, getting a feel for the unfamiliar sax. Moments later, he started playing Boyz II Men's "I'll Make Love to You." For the entire summer of '94, the song could be heard coming from his sister's bedroom 24/7.

As he serenaded the couple, his eyes found Phylicia. She sat with her elbow propped up on the table, chin in her hand. A wistful smile graced her lips.

Jamal was suddenly struck with a sense of déjà vu. It was in an atmosphere like this one that he'd first started to fall for her. He hadn't even known her all that well at Mya and Corey's wedding, yet he'd been drawn to her. Later that night, as they'd talked about every insignificant thing under the moon, he'd realized that she was the type of woman he could easily see himself spending the rest of his life with.

He blew out the last few notes of the song, shrugging off the bevy of applause from the audience with a modest wave. He leaned over and whispered something to the band leader before walking over to Lauryn and his new brother-in-law. He enveloped them both in a hug, and kissed his sister's cheek.

God, she looked happy. He could only hope to find such happiness one day.

With that thought in mind, Jamal headed straight for Phylicia.

"That was lovely," she said.

"Thank you," Jamal answered. He held his hand out. "This next dance is for us."

Her head tilted to the side, her brows raised in question. As the song he'd requested started, a slow smile spread across her face. She captured his hand and allowed him to guide her onto the dance floor. Phylicia rested her cheek against his shoulder as they swayed back and forth.

"This is the song that played for the bridal party dance at Mya and Corey's wedding," she said.

Jamal nodded. "It was the first song we ever danced to."

"I can't believe you remembered that," she said.

"That song played in my head for days after the wedding. I couldn't get it out of my mind." He pulled slightly away and peered down at her. "You really don't have a clue how much you affected me that night, do you, Phylicia? I fell for you. Hard. And I've been falling ever since."

She stared up at him, her eyes filled with the same emotion that was tightening his chest. "I'm falling, too," she admitted in a soft voice. "I'm not sure I can fall much deeper."

The air between them vibrated with an intense energy. It was as if everyone else had disappeared, leaving the two of them to savor this experience in their own private universe. This song, this place, this moment; it was just for them.

"I'm in love with you," Jamal said. He hadn't meant to say it; the words came out involuntarily. But now that he'd put them out there, he wouldn't take them back.

Phylicia just stared at him, her expression unreadable.

Something close to panic clawed up Jamal's throat. It was too soon. She was good and spooked; he could feel it in the way her body stiffened against him.

She dropped her gaze to his chest. "If I tell you the same thing, you have to promise you won't hurt me," she whispered, her soft voice saturated with uncertainty.

"I told you before that I would never hurt you, Phylicia." He captured her chin between his fingers and lifted her gaze to meet his. "I'm not Kevin. Don't make me pay for his mistakes."

"No, you're not Kevin," she agreed. "I know you would never hurt me the way he did."

The song ended, but Jamal didn't move. He refused to leave this spot until he knew how she truly felt about him.

When Phylicia's gaze met his, the sheen of unshed tears in her eyes caused his throat to painfully constrict. The vulnerability radiating from her was such a contradiction to her usually tough exterior.

"I think I'm in love with you, too, Jamal," she finally said, then she shook her head. "No, I don't think it. I know it."

His chest expanded with the deep breath he heaved, the swell of emotion threatening to overwhelm him. Jamal leaned forward and pressed a soft, gentle kiss to her lips. He wanted nothing more than to stand in this one spot, kissing her forever.

"Will Mother have another wedding to plan soon?"

A smile crept up the sides of Jamal's mouth as he turned to his sister, who stood a few feet behind them.

"You're such a brat," he teased. Still holding on to Phylicia with one hand, he brought his sister in for a hug, pressing a kiss to the top of her head. "Did I tell you how amazing you look today? I'm so happy for you, Lauryn."

Tears glistened in her eyes. "Thank you for coming," she said. "My day would not have been complete without you."

Swallowing past the lump of emotion lodged in his throat, Jamal smiled and said, "Thank Phylicia. Somehow she managed to convince me."

"Really?" Lauryn asked, a curious hike to

her brow. "There's actually a woman on earth who can get through Jamal's thick skull? Who knew?"

"Hey," Jamal protested as Phylicia and Lauryn both laughed.

With one last kiss to his cheek, his sister left the two of them so she could greet other guests.

Lacing her fingers behind his neck, Phylicia smiled into his eyes. "Your sister is a character."

"She was the bane of my existence growing up."

"Stop it," Phylicia chastised. "Your family is great, so warm and down-to-earth. I won't lie — they are the complete opposite of what I expected."

"What did you expect?"

"Uppity rich people," she said with a frankness that was all Phylicia.

Jamal chuckled. "We're pretty grounded," he said, settling his hands on her waist and guiding her in a gentle sway to the soft ballad coming from the band.

"They are lovely. Including your dad," she added after a pause. "I talked to him earlier, when you went to the car to get your sister's gift."

"Don't," he said.

"He hates this estrangement, Jamal."

"Don't get in the middle of this, Phylicia."

"What's the point of keeping up this dispute if the two of you are both miserable?"

"Who says I'm miserable?"

Her gorgeous lips thinned in annoyance. "Why don't you just hear him out? Don't lose any more time fighting, Jamal. You never know how much you're going to have left."

God, she was stubborn.

"Leave it alone," Jamal beseeched. "I'm begging you, Phylicia. Just leave it alone."

"But —"

Jamal shut her up the only way he knew how, capturing the back of her head and crushing his mouth to hers. She fought his kiss for only a moment before Jamal felt her body relax against him and her lips slowly open. He would give anything to engage in a full-on, open-mouth kiss with her, but he knew it would leave him aroused and aching. And since they had a two-hour drive before they would get to a bed, he had to stop before things went too far.

Phylicia tore her mouth from his. The censure in her frown was ruined by the desire smoldering in her eyes. "You do not play fair," she accused.

"I never claimed I would," he returned.

"This conversation isn't over, Jamal."

Instead of arguing with her, Jamal gave her another swift kiss and guided her back to their table. The day had been too perfect; he would not spoil it with talk of his father.

Moments later, Lauryn and Michael bade their guests farewell, but the party was far from over. The ten-piece band was replaced by a popular local DJ, and the mood switched from sedate wedding reception to nightclub-style party.

As he and Phylicia danced the rest of the night away, Jamal knew there was no way they would make it back to Sedona tonight. Not only had he indulged in one too many drinks from the free-flowing bar, but after feeling Phylicia's body brush up against his all night, he knew he would not be able to sustain a two-hour drive without having her. They would end up parked on the side of Interstate 17, stripping each other out of their clothes.

"I think it's time to get out of here," he whispered in her ear as they swayed back and forth to Maxwell's "Lifetime."

"I think you're right," she answered. "I'm not sure I can go much longer before I just pass out."

"Oh, you're not going to sleep," Jamal

warned her.

The smile that tipped up the corners of her mouth was carnal, and set his blood to high boil.

Jamal took her by the hand and headed straight for the front desk, booking a night's stay at the Biltmore. As soon as they entered their room, Jamal took her lips in a kiss that resonated throughout his entire body. Within moments of closing the door to the suite, he had her naked and spread out over the bed. With one goal in mind, Jamal proceeded to turn her body inside out. Before the night was over, this woman would know that she belonged to him in every single way.

"I still cannot believe how beautiful this place is," Phil said, her eyes gazing out the passenger window of the rental car. "Makes me sad to think about leaving."

"All it takes is a phone call to the airline. We can tack on a couple of days."

"No, we can't," she said. "We need to get Belle Maison finished before Thursday, because I am not spending my Thanksgiving working."

"Let me guess, you want to spend it watching all the football games."

"Shut up." She swatted his arm. "The

furniture is arriving tomorrow, and your first guests will check in next week. Oh!" She twisted in her seat to face him. "I completely forgot to tell you this. Mya left a voice mail on my cell phone last night while we were at the wedding. She said that *Gulf-scapes Magazine* has agreed to feature Gauthier, and they're going to come down for the Christmas in Gauthier celebration to take photos."

"Whoa, that's pretty huge. I'm surprised news like that didn't send her into labor," Jamal said with a chuckle.

"Maybe if we can convince them to stay at Belle Maison, they'll throw a little extra advertising our way," she said.

A warm smile traveled across Jamal's lips. "I like the way you include yourself when you talk about the bed-and-breakfast."

She hesitated a moment. "I guess it's because we've been working so closely together on it."

"Is that the only reason?" he asked. He reached across the center console and captured her hand. "I was hoping it was because you were starting to see yourself as a part of it, and not just someone I hired to help. Because you mean a lot more to Belle Maison, Phylicia. And to me."

His words caused a maelstrom of giddiness, excitement and downright panic to swirl in the pit of her stomach. He caressed the back of her hand with his thumb, rubbing it back and forth.

"I meant what I said last night, Phylicia. I'm in love with you. And it's not going to go away once we're done working on the house. I'm in this. Completely."

Her throat tightened with emotion. "What are you saying, Jamal?"

"What do you think I'm saying? I'm asking if you're in this, too. Do you see the two of us running Belle Maison together? Living our lives together? Maybe even getting married, having children?"

Oh, God, she could absolutely see it. All of it.

Phil's free hand shook as she brought it up to her trembling lips. After everything she had been through over these past few years, a part of her was afraid to acknowledge what appeared to be true happiness within her reach.

"I can see it," she said. "And I *do* want all of it. With you."

Jamal let out a deep breath she had no idea he had been holding. An enormous smile broke out over his face. He leaned over and kissed her for so long that Phil was sure he would veer off the road. He drove one-handed for the remainder of the drive, his other hand never letting go of hers.

Phil had been afraid to even imagine that she could ever feel this kind of contentment again. Even though the burdens were still there — the pressure from the bank, dealing with her mother's illness and the rising cost of her care — the peace that settled over her made them all seem inconsequential. With Jamal at her side, giving her his love and support, Phil knew she would get through it all.

They turned off the highway and onto the road leading to the Creekside Bed-and-Breakfast. As the house came into view, Jamal's grip loosened on her hand.

"What the hell?" he asked.

Phil spotted what had caught his attention. A shiny black Bentley was parked in front of the inn's entrance.

Jamal slammed on the brakes and threw the car into Park. "How in the hell did he know we were here?"

Her heart pounding, Phil sucked in a deep breath. "I told him," she admitted.

His head whipped around, his usually soft eyes shooting daggers at her.

"I told you that we spoke at the reception yesterday," she explained. "All he could talk about was how much he regrets what happened between the two of you."

"Dammit, Phylicia." A muscle jumped in his jaw. "I told you to stay out of it."

The Bentley's driver's side door opened, and Lawrence Johnson stepped out, dressed in a tailored suit. Jamal's nostrils flared, and his grip on the steering wheel tightened.

"You had no right to bring him here," he bit out. He opened the door and stalked right past his father.

Phil got out of the car and ran after him. She gave Mr. Johnson a hasty greeting but didn't stop. When she got to the room, she found Jamal pacing back and forth in front of the bed.

"I was only trying to help, Jamal. I know firsthand what happens when you allow something to come between you and your family. It can eat you alive. I don't want you to suffer with the same regrets I've dealt with these past three years."

He pointed toward the door. "You don't know anything about what happened between me and that man."

"I know you and your father both probably said things that neither of you meant, and by not talking it out, you've only made things worse. It's the same thing that happened with me and my dad."

"I don't give a damn about what happened between you and your dad!" he shouted.

Phil took a step back, the ugliness of his words slapping her in the face, the ferociousness in his voice sending a tremor of unease down her spine.

"This had *nothing* to do with you," Jamal lashed out. "You think I'm going to just forget everything and play nice because that's what *you* think is best for me? I've spent my entire damn life doing what he wanted me to do. I sure as hell won't let you come in and try to dictate what I do, too."

"I'm not trying to tell you what to do," she protested.

"The hell you're not!" His voice nearly shook the windows. "I told you I wanted nothing to do with that man, yet you go behind my back and tell him where to find me? You should have just stayed the hell out of it like I told you."

Phil tried several times before she could swallow past the lump in her throat. She blinked rapidly, hoping to avoid the wounded tears that threatened to escape.

When she spoke, she barely recognized her own voice. "You're right," she managed to get out. "It was none of my business. I'm sorry."

Jamal stopped pacing and stared directly into her eyes. He didn't acknowledge her apology, but just stood there, fury radiating from his rigid frame. The rage sparkling like fire in his eyes was unlike anything she'd ever seen in him.

There was a knock at the door.

"Can I come in?" came Lawrence Johnson's formidable baritone.

Phil didn't think Jamal could look any angrier than he had just a moment ago, but the sound of his father's voice brought his fury to a new level.

She turned and walked over to the door, opening it just wide enough to slip out of the suite. The look on Lawrence Johnson's face would have broken her heart if his son hadn't already crushed it with his cruel, unforgivable words.

"I'm sorry," she said.

The man expelled a harsh breath. "So am I," he said. "He takes after his father, even though you'd never get him to admit it. We're both stubborn asses." The older man gave her a sheepish look. "I'm sorry if this has caused problems between the two of you. I couldn't help but overhear."

Phil shook her head. "It's okay."

But it was anything *but* okay.

It was exactly what she'd feared — raw,

gut-wrenching despair at the hands of the man she'd trusted with her most fragile, most treasured possession. Her heart.

"I'm sorry you drove all this way for nothing," Phil told him.

"It was worth the drive if it meant finally getting past this with Jamal. I'll get through to him eventually." Mr. Johnson, with eyes so much like his son's, took her hands in his. "Thank you for trying."

"You're welcome," Phil returned.

He pulled her in for a hug, giving her an extra, reassuring squeeze. Phil closed her eyes tightly, but she couldn't help the tears that began to flow.

How could Jamal not see how lucky he was to still have his father?

He released her from the hug, but he didn't let go of her hands. Instead, he gripped them tighter and looked directly into her eyes. "Don't allow my son's stubbornness to come between the two of you. Just give him some time to cool off. Don't let him give you the silent treatment for too long, either."

"We have a six o'clock flight back to Louisiana. He won't be able to avoid me for long."

"Travel safely," he said, then he turned and headed back for the entrance to the inn.

Phil stood outside the suite's door for several minutes, trying to collect herself. She pulled in deep breath after increasingly deep breath, shoring up her nerve before reentering the room. But when she went back in, it was empty. The French doors to the patio were opened, the sheer curtains billowing slightly in the breeze. She walked out onto the private patio and spotted Jamal standing at the edge of the creek.

Phil made her way down the pebbled trail that stretched from their room to the creek. She stopped a few feet behind him, staring at his solid back as he stood with his feet braced apart, his shoulders rigid, his hands stuffed into the pockets of his black pants.

"He's gone," she called in a hushed voice.

Her pronouncement was met with silence, the gurgle of the creek and squawk of a bird flying overhead the only sounds.

"Our flight leaves in less than four hours," she said. "If we're going to make it back to Phoenix in time, we need to start packing now."

A long, pregnant pause stretched between them before Jamal finally spoke.

"I called a car service to pick you up in an hour," he said.

The dull ache that had settled in her chest mushroomed into a cloud of hurt that enveloped her entire being. Phil wrapped her arms around her middle in an attempt to stop the pain from pummeling her to the ground.

"Don't do this, Jamal," she said in an anguished whisper. "You promised me you wouldn't hurt me."

His back remained rigid as he continued to stare out over the water.

"I'm sorry for overstepping," Phil maintained, her voice breaking over the words. "But that is no reason for you to do this. Don't shut me out, Jamal."

His shoulders rose slightly with the breath he took.

"You should pack," he said.

Phil pulled her trembling lips between her teeth. She stared at him until his body was completely blurred by the tears that welled in her eyes.

The tears cascaded down her cheeks as she returned to the suite and packed her bags. They streamed in earnest as she rode in the backseat of the hired car, as she boarded the plane in Phoenix and, hours later, as she lay her head on her pillow back at her house in Gauthier.

CHAPTER 15

Jamal sat on the edge of the rock-strewn cliff, looking out over the red clay that stretched for miles around him. He'd give anything to have his sax in his hand. He needed the solace that came with losing himself in a piece of music.

He rubbed at the ache that had resided in his chest for the past five days. It had started the moment he'd sent Phylicia away. No matter what he tried, the pain refused to let up.

Jamal pitched a rock into the hollow vastness that lay before him. He'd been so damn philosophic this week, he was driving himself crazy. But he could not escape the symbolism. The never-ending stretch of nothingness mimicked his life to perfection.

He'd reached a new low point. The most amazing woman he would ever have the luxury of knowing had told him she loved him, and he'd sent her packing.

Here he was, only a couple of hours from his family, and yesterday he'd spent Thanksgiving with two strangers at a bed-and-breakfast in Lake Montezuma. What did that say about the state his life was in? What did that say about him?

That he was a damn coward.

The ugly truth had hit him square in the gut as soon as he'd retuned to the suite he'd shared with Phylicia back in Sedona. She'd tried to save him from suffering the same fate she'd met, but he'd been too much of a coward to face the truth of her words. Too afraid to accept his role in the mess he'd made of his relationship with his father.

Jamal figured it was easier to just walk away, to lay the blame for his shattered relationships at everyone else's feet. It was his father's lack of respect that had caused this chasm to stretch between them. It was Phylicia's dogged insistence at sticking her nose where it didn't belong that had caused him to send her away.

But it was his own stubbornness that had him here, all alone, his mind reverberating with all the things he'd fought valiantly to keep at bay. The truth was laid bare now, demanding an audience, and Jamal could do nothing but see it for what it was. Phylicia had been right. He could spend the rest of his life coming up with projects to keep him occupied so that he could put off opening his firm. The only thing that had been stopping him was *him.*

And his gut-wrenching, soul-stealing fear of failing.

It was that fear of proving his father's prophecy right — that he would have to come crawling back a failure — that was at the root of his fear.

But what if he didn't fail?

What if he finally put to use those ideas he'd been stockpiling for years and they actually worked? He'd crunched the numbers countless times; he knew the tide was shifting and that making older homes more eco-friendly was the wave of the future. What was he waiting for? Some other architectural outfit to step in and make a success of his ideas?

"What in the hell is wrong with you?" Jamal cursed. He pushed himself up from where he'd been perched on the cliff and quickly made his way down the side of the foothill. As soon as he got in his car, he pulled up the number for his Realtor in New Orleans, hoping she wasn't out scouring the day-after Thanksgiving sales. When she answered on the second ring, Jamal's chest nearly burst with relief.

"Is the house on Saint Charles Avenue still available?" he asked.

"Yes, it is," she said.

"I want it. I'll be in New Orleans by tonight. Do whatever you can to make the sale happen quickly. I want to be in there as soon as possible."

He returned to the bed-and-breakfast he'd found in Lake Montezuma and packed his things, booking a return flight home as he shoved his clothes into his bags.

Soon, Jamal was driving south, making his way back to Phoenix. But instead of continuing straight on I-17 toward Sky Harbor International, Jamal took the exit at Camelback Road and headed east toward the suburb of Arcadia.

He was done running away. Phylicia was right. He didn't want to live with regrets, not when he still had a chance at making things right.

Jamal pulled up to the gates of the home he'd grown up in, modest by the standards of some of the mansions springing up in other parts of the city. He dialed in the key code, a measure of comfort washing over him at the knowledge that the numbers had not changed.

He entered the house using the key he'd kept stuffed in his wallet — the key his mother had insisted he have, even though he hadn't lived in this house in nearly a decade. His mother was in the foyer, watering the large, fresh flower arrangement that sat in the middle of a round marble table.

She twisted around and gasped. "Jamal?"

"Hi, Mom," he answered.

"How . . . why?" She walked up to him. "What are you still doing in Arizona? I thought you left the day after the wedding."

Shame washed over him. Jamal didn't want to tell her he'd been here the entire week and had purposely missed Thanksgiving yesterday. It would hurt her too much. Instead, he got right to the point of his unexpected detour.

"Where is he?" Jamal asked.

"Jamal, please, no more fighting," she pleaded.

"I don't want to fight with him," he told her.

The hope that sprung in her eyes made her look ten years younger, and Jamal was hit with the reality of the toll this rift with his father had taken on the rest of the family.

"He's in his office," his mother said. Jamal started for the marble stairs that led to the second floor, but his mother stopped him before he could take a step. "Thank you," she said. "Thank you for coming back."

Jamal pressed a quick kiss to her forehead. "You're welcome," he said. "And I promise never to stay away this long again."

He took the stairs two at a time. Jamal stopped short as he came upon the dark wood door of his father's home office. He gave it two short raps.

"Come in," came the deep voice from the other side of the door.

Jamal pushed it open and stared at his father. "I think we need to talk," he said.

"This is nice, isn't it, Agatha?"

"Yes, it is," Phil replied. She leaned over and peered at her mother's canvas. Her rendering of the small gazebo surrounded by flowers was nearly an exact replication of the actual structure that stood before them in the serenity garden on the grounds of Mossy Oaks.

She tilted her head to the side as she gazed at her mother. "I'm so grateful you can still paint."

"I don't know for how much longer. I'm getting old. Arthritis may soon set in." Her mother's cagey smile warmed Phil's heart.

"You've been robbed of so much," Phil whispered. "I think God will let you paint for a while longer."

Her mother set her brush in the easel's tray and walked over to her. "Is that your young man?" Sabina asked as she stared at Phil's painting.

Most of the portrait was still in outline form, an outline she'd sketched from memory. "It is," Phil answered.

"I hope he comes back to see me soon. He is a very nice young man, Aggie. I'm so happy you found someone like him."

Phil just smiled. She knew if she tried to talk those damn tears would start flowing.

They stayed in the garden for another hour, their conversation jumping from one decade to another. As usual, Phil tried to follow as best she could, and she embellished whenever necessary. When the nurse came to retrieve Sabina for afternoon exercise, Phil bade her mother goodbye with a kiss on the cheek and a promise to return in a few days.

On her way out of Mossy Oaks, Phil stopped in the director's office.

"She seems to be doing well," she said to Dr. Beckman.

"We haven't had any more episodes," he told her. His face took on a thoughtful, contemplative look. "Can you close the door? I'd like to speak to you privately, Ms. Phillips."

Fear threaded down Phil's spine. "Is there a problem?" she asked.

"No. Actually, this may be the best thing that's happened in quite some time." He gestured for her to take a seat. When she was settled, he continued. "There is an experimental study being conducted at LSU's medical school, and they've contacted Mossy Oaks for study subjects. I believe your mother would be a good candidate."

Phil's heart started pounding against her rib cage, curiosity and hope flooding her brain as the facility's director gave her an overview of what the study would entail.

"This wouldn't cure her," Dr. Beckman was quick to point out. "But, if successful, it could significantly slow the progression of her disease."

Phil brought a trembling hand to her mouth.

"I don't want to get your hopes up," he cautioned. "Remember, it's experimental, and there are no guarantees, but it's something to consider."

"Whatever can be done, do it," she said. "I need her here as long as possible. Even if she thinks I'm my aunt Agatha."

Dr. Beckman nodded and smiled. "Good. I'll keep you abreast of the study. And when it's time, I'll have the paperwork for you to sign."

Phil couldn't help it. She stood, walked over to the director and wrapped her arms around him. "Thank you so much for all you do."

Even if she had to sell her house and live on the streets, she would do whatever she had to do to keep her mother at Mossy Oaks. Moving her from this place and its amazing staff wasn't an option.

Her cell phone started ringing as she made her way to the parking lot. Phil recognized the number; it was the real estate company she'd hired to sell the properties she owned in Maplesville. Dread climbed up her spine. What was it now? A fire? Vandals? Termite infestation?

"Hello?" Phil answered, preparing herself for the worst.

"Hello, Ms. Phillips, this is Tiffany Conner with Conner Realty. I have some good news for you."

Phil stopped in her tracks. "Yes?" she asked, too afraid to hope.

"We have a buyer for one of your properties," the woman said.

"Oh, my God," Phil breathed. Her knees nearly buckled with the relief that crashed through her. "Are you serious?"

"I sure am. A husband and wife and their beautiful twin girls. They just moved down from Jackson, Mississippi. They said the house is perfect for them."

"That's just . . . it's wonderful," Phil said, still breathless. The anxiety that had been weighing down on her chest like a boulder slowly began to lift.

"Congratulations," Tiffany Conner said. "Let's hope we can move the other two houses soon."

"Let's hope," Phil replied. She made plans to meet with the Realtor at her office tomorrow to go over the details of the impending sale.

After she ended the call, Phil sat in her truck for several long moments, staring at Mossy Oaks' beautiful chateau-style exterior. An overwhelming sense of peace settled into her bones as she thought about the doctors and staff and how her mother would now be able to remain under their care for the foreseeable future.

"God, thank you," Phil whispered, her shoulders sagging with relief.

Unfortunately, the peaceful calm that had enveloped her didn't last very long. As she traveled along Highway 21 on her way back to Gauthier, the aching in her chest kicked up once again. She had lived with it for well over a week, through Thanksgiving. It just wouldn't go away.

She exited the highway, coming to the juncture at Pine Street and Highway 436. She wanted to turn left toward her house. She could hole up in her big, empty bed and not surface for days. Maybe even weeks.

But she wasn't one to hide, nor did she shirk her responsibilities.

Phil turned left and headed for Loring Avenue. The restoration on Belle Maison was nearly complete. She had no idea when Jamal would return — or even if he would return. Maybe Tiffany Conner would show up here in a few days with a For Sale sign. But Phil had been hired to do a job. She was going to get it done.

She parked in the driveway and headed for the downstairs bathroom. She would put the finishing touches on the trimming she'd restored and then take an inventory of what was left to do before guests began arriving in a few days.

As she worked, Phil thought about how her views on the house had changed over the past couple of months. When she'd first started the job, the thought of a host of strangers breezing in and out of Belle Maison made her physically ill. But as she'd worked to restore the house to its former glory, she came to the realization that this house was too special to remain uninhabited. Her great-great-grandfather's hard labor was meant to be enjoyed. She was looking forward to seeing the reaction of guests when they crossed the grand home's threshold.

Hurt pierced her chest as Phil accepted the likelihood that she probably wouldn't get to see their faces. She'd pictured herself here with Jamal, inviting people into Belle Maison, showing off her family's legacy with pride. She'd imagined the two of them sharing the history of the house and the story of how they had restored it. Even how Jamal had updated it with his quirky green technology.

"You can get that out of your head," she said to the empty room.

She'd allowed herself to be pulled into this fantasy, and it had come back to bite her square in the behind. This was Jamal's house. They were not the happy little couple who would spend their days running a cozy bed-and-breakfast. She was Jamal Johnson's employee, nothing more.

She would finish her work here and get back to pulling herself out of debt. The money from the property that sold in Maplesville would help tremendously. If she was able to get a steady stream of restoration work, she would be on the right track. Except for this broken heart she was still nursing. She had a feeling it wouldn't be healed anytime soon.

"You shouldn't have stuck your nose in where it didn't belong," Phil reprimanded herself. It didn't matter that it was with the best of intentions.

None of it mattered. She was here to do a job. She'd allowed herself to get swept away by Jamal's charm and his incredible body, and now she was paying the price. She'd been through something similar with Kevin and had survived. She could do it again.

Although, Phil had the foreboding feeling that it would take much, *much* longer to get over Jamal. At least she hadn't had to see Kevin after he'd picked up and run off to California. If Jamal decided to return to Gauthier, avoiding him would be nearly impossible in this small town.

But the fact that she'd fallen much harder for Jamal than she had for Kevin — than she had for *any* man — was the major difference when it came to the anticipated recovery time for this particular broken heart. This recovery would take forever.

She gave herself a mental shake and got back to work. The quicker she was done here, the quicker she could move on.

An hour later, as she wiped down the mantel in the parlor, an eerie feeling tiptoed down Phil's spine. Seconds later, she heard a rumbling coming up the driveway. She left the dust cloth on the mantel and went out the front door onto the porch.

Her heart stuttered in her chest as Jamal's black-and-chrome pickup truck pulled to a stop and the driver's side door opened. When he stepped out, Phil's heart ached at the sight of him.

Time stood still as they stared at each other across the expanse of the front yard. After several long, uncomfortable moments, Jamal broke the silence.

"I wasn't expecting to find you here," he said.

Phil had to clear her throat before speaking. "I have a job to do," she said.

He closed the door to the truck and took a few steps forward. He stuffed his hands in his front jeans pockets then pulled them out again and ran a palm over his head and down his face. His fidgeting was unnerving, but Phil maintained her composure as best she could.

"Is that the only reason you're here?" he asked. "Are you leaving once the job is done?"

"I figured that's what you would want," she managed to get out.

Jamal shook his head; the sincerity shining through his eyes pierced her heart. "No," he said. "I don't want you to leave, Phylicia."

Phil's chest expanded with the deep breath she pulled in. She was afraid to read too much into his words, afraid to hope. In a few strides, Jamal was on the porch, standing before her.

"I owe you an apology," he said.

Phil shook her head. "No, you don't."

"Yes, I do," he insisted. "I have never spoken to a woman the way I spoke to you. Phylicia, I can't begin to tell you how sorry I am for how I treated you back in Arizona. I'll never forgive myself for sending you away the way I did."

"I stuck my nose in where it didn't belong," Phil said.

"Don't make excuses for me. You were trying to make me see what I was too stubborn to see for myself. You were trying to give me my family back."

Phil nodded. She couldn't speak even if she tried.

"You were right." After a beat, he said, "I talked to my father."

Instant tears sprang to Phil's eyes, her throat clogging with emotion.

Jamal gave a slight shrug. "We didn't instantly hug and put the past behind us, but things . . . they're better. We're going to work on our relationship."

"Oh, Jamal, I'm so happy for you," Phil said. She pulled her trembling lips between her teeth, trying her hardest to rein in her emotions. "That's all I wanted for you," she continued. "I swear I wasn't trying to intrude or force you to do something you didn't want to do. I just didn't want you to live with the same regrets I live with every day."

"I know," he said, taking her hands and placing a kiss upon her fingers. "And because of you, I won't. Because of you, I'm moving forward and not wasting another minute hiding from my future. I bought the house on Saint Charles Avenue, Phylicia. J. Johnson Architectural Design will open its doors by the spring."

Phil grabbed his face between her hands and pulled it toward her. "I am so proud of you," she whispered against his lips. "It's going to be amazing. Just wait."

"I know it will," he said. He leaned forward and pressed his lips against hers. "Thank you for not giving up on this house, or on me. Thank you for challenging me to be a better man."

Her eyes slid shut, the love pouring through her suffocating in its intensity. "I love you so much, Jamal," Phil said.

"Not as much as I love you," he returned. "I never thought this kind of love was possible, Phylicia. And it wasn't, not until I found you."

EPILOGUE

Using her foot to slide open the pocket door that led to Belle Maison's dining room, Phil carried in another batch of homemade biscuits and a pot of steaming coffee, replenishing the cups of the ten guests seated around the large table. The bed-and-breakfast had been open only for a week, but already it felt like a warm, inviting home that had never been unoccupied.

"Can I get you anything else?" she asked one of the women who was part of a trio of friends from Pensacola.

"You can get me about five jars of these strawberry preserves," the woman answered.

"Sorry," Phil answered with a laugh. "It's not for sale."

"Well, it should be," the woman said. "It's one of the best I've ever had. You should package this and sell it. You'd make a killing."

"Thank you." Phil beamed. "It's my

grandmother's recipe. She used to make it right here in the kitchen of Belle Maison. I'll bring out more, along with some of the honey. It's also made here in Gauthier."

"I just love this little town," the woman said.

"There's a lot to love about it," Phil said, pride blossoming in her chest.

She cleared the plates of several of the guests and carried them back into the kitchen, depositing the dirty dishes in the dishwasher — one of her concessions to modernizing the Victorian. If the reservations continued to pour in the way they had over the past couple of weeks, Belle Maison's new caretaker, who was scheduled to arrive next week, would have enough on her hands without adding hand washing dirty dishes to her plate.

A part of her resented the thought of someone else coming in to run the B&B. This week had been challenging, but Phil couldn't deny that she'd enjoyed it. Seeing the faces of the guests as they took in all of the nuances of her family's home was so satisfying. She'd loved giving tours this week, imparting anecdotes about what it was like to grow up here.

She'd even enjoyed the cooking, something she hadn't done in a long time.

Jamal came up behind her and buried his face against her neck, pressing a quick kiss to the sensitive spot under her ear. "I had no idea you knew your way around the kitchen," he said. "I think it's sexy."

"Sexy, huh?"

"Oh, yeah," he said. He nibbled her ear. "You know what would be even sexier? If you were wearing those denim overalls you work in. But just the overalls. No shirt underneath."

"Um, that would leave me pretty exposed." Phil laughed even as a seductive little tremor of need raced across her skin.

"That's the point."

Phil slapped him on the arm and handed him the jar of strawberry preserves and the honey from Claude Babineaux's honey farm. "Bring this out to your guests, and remind them that the van will be arriving in a few minutes to bring them on their tour of downtown Gauthier."

"Will you be waiting for me in those overalls when I clear the people out of this house?" he asked. "We haven't christened the kitchen yet, have we?"

They'd christened every room in the B&B — some twice.

"You know what?" Jamal continued. "On second thought, forget the overalls. Just you on the kitchen table will work for me."

The naughty tremors that rushed down Phil's spine made her itch with anticipation, but her body's demands would have to wait.

"No fooling around today," Phil told him. "Mya is waiting for me. The civic association is putting the finishing touches on the Christmas decorations in Heritage Park. I promised her I would help."

Jamal's incredulous frown wrung out a laugh from her. "You would pick hanging decorations over wild sex on the kitchen table?" he asked.

Phil's body released a mournful sigh, but whatever she didn't get to experience on the kitchen table would be more than made up for in Jamal's bed tonight. Or her bed. It didn't matter which one they used. For the past two weeks they had not spent a single night alone, and Phil had no desire to ever do so again. She needed this man in her life. And, thank God, he seemed to need her just as much. The engagement ring he'd placed on her finger a few days ago said it all.

"Fine," he said. He leaned over and placed a kiss on her lips. "Are we going to pick up your mom this afternoon?"

"Yes," Phil answered. "Dr. Beckman thinks she will be okay for a few hours. It's been a long time since she's seen Gauthier. Maybe it'll spark something in her memory."

"I hope so," Jamal said with another kiss. She would never, ever get tired of his kisses.

He reached his hand behind her and gave her butt a healthy pat. "Leave this mess. I'll take care of it. I want you to finish up with Mya so we can have a little free time before we have to pick up your mom."

Phil shook her head. "You really can't wait until tonight?"

He shrugged. "Probably, but give me a good reason why I should."

Phil's brows lifted. "You know what? I can't think of one." She slapped him on the behind. "I'll clear the table. And, Jamal?" She reached over and took the jar of honey from his hand. "I can think of a better use for this."

A wickedly sexy smile broke out across his face.

"God, I love an insatiable woman."

ABOUT THE AUTHOR

Farrah Rochon had dreams as a teenager of becoming a fashion designer, until she discovered she would be expected to wear something other than jeans to work every day. Thankfully, the coffee shop where she writes does not have a dress code.

When Farrah is not penning stories, the avid sports fan feeds her addiction to football by attending New Orleans Saints games.

The employees of Thorndike Press hope you have enjoyed this Large Print book. All our Thorndike, Wheeler, and Kennebec Large Print titles are designed for easy reading, and all our books are made to last. Other Thorndike Press Large Print books are available at your library, through selected bookstores, or directly from us.

For information about titles, please call:
(800) 223-1244

or visit our Web site at:
http://gale.cengage.com/thorndike

To share your comments, please write:
Publisher
Thorndike Press
10 Water St., Suite 310
Waterville, ME 04901